THE NORWEGIAN CHRISTMAS MARRIAGE PLOT

MARRIAGE PLOT

A SWEET ROMANTIC COMEDY

AUSTIN RYAN

ABOUT THE BOOK

I've known Ragnhild since she was a blue-eyed preschooler with a halo of red hair and chubby fingers clutched in mine.

Eighteen years later she's still my best friend and her ideas are as crazy as they were then.

When she stages a wedding to make her co-worker jealous, there isn't enough coffee and *smultringer* in the world to convince me to help some random guy steal my best friend's heart.

But there is a girl.

A girl with red hair that calls to my hands and a smile that makes my heart feel light and buoyant. A girl I can't say no to—even as she asks me to play the pretend groom in her make-believe wedding.

But as gingersnap hearts are hung in the windows of the old farmhouse and Christmas Eve draws nearer, I'm not so sure I can do it.

Because while this upcoming wedding is fake, my feelings for Ragnhild are very, very real. And as long as the sizzling chemistry between us rivals the heat of the *Jøtul* stove in the house, I'm nowhere near ready to give up.

The Norwegian Christmas Marriage Plot is a sweet romantic

comedy with all the chemistry, none of the spice, and a host of Norwegian Christmas food and traditions at the center. It rates a 3 or 4 on the RCRS scale.

To Besten,

Per Skjæveland

5/23/1933 – 10/22/2020

for passing on your humor, your
love of books and reading, and for
handing me the books that shaped
my writing voice.

For Kieran Benjamin Ryan,
because I write it all for you.

PRONUNCIATION GUIDE

For all of my readers who requested this in the first version of this book, here is the pronunciation guide:

Thorleif = THAWR-layf (Old Norse for descendant of Thor)
Vaage = VAW-geh
Ragnhild = RAHGN-hild (Old Norse for counsel in battle)
Bestemor = BESTEH-mohr (Norwegian for grandmother)
Mor = MOHR (Norwegian for mother)

NORWEGIAN WORD LIST

Bunad = traditional Norwegian dress and national costume. The style and colors of *bunads* vary depending on the area of the country where the dress originated. Ragnhild's *bunad* depicted in this story is based on the one my grandmother sewed for me and originates from Sunnhordland in Norway. Ragnhild wears a red waist, white linen shirt, embroidered stomacher and belt, silver brooch and laces, black skirts, and woven apron in blue, white, and black.

Thorleif's *bunad* is also based on the Sunnhordland *bunad*. This variation has a double-breasted red waistcoat, white linen shirt, black jacket, and knee-length breeches. He also wears white knit stockings, colorful braided garters, and silver-buckled shoes.

Gløgg = spicy Christmas drink similar to wassail or mulled wine, served hot with raisins and chopped almonds.

Havreflarn = thin, crispy, caramelized oatmeal cookies.

Julemenn = sweet cookie leavened (and flavored) with ammonium bicarbonate. I highly recommend holding your breath when you open the oven to take these cookies out because your eyes will water and passing out puts a damper on the Christmas preparations (can you actually pass out from this? I don't know, but it sure feels like it).

Jøtul stove = 'jøtul' is an old Norwegian word for troll, and also the name of a worldwide producer of Norwegian cast iron stoves.

Kokosmakroner = coconut macaroons, my maternal grandfather's favorite.

Kringle = traditional Norwegian pastry made with fine wheat flour, and sometimes raisins and succades. The glaze is made from water and powdered sugar.

Lusekofte = knit sweater in traditional patterns.

Lussekatt = traditional Norwegian pastry prepared for St. Lucia Day on December 13th. Saffron (or turmeric) gives these sweet rolls their yellow color. They are made into traditional shapes, and decorated with raisins.

Pepperkaker = in this book, I've used the word 'gingersnaps' to translate the Norwegian Christmas cookie, *pepperkake*, but they are, of course, somewhat different cookies. Pepperkaker sometimes contain pepper, but more often ginger, cinnamon, cardamom, and cloves. They may also have been named so because spices in general were referred to as 'pepper.' The dough is rolled thin and cut out with cookie cutters. The traditional shapes are men, women, and pigs, but in growing up we also had angels, camels, horses, boats, and trains.

Romjul = the week between Christmas Eve (December 24th) and New Year's Day (January 1st), considered an important part of the Norwegian Christmas celebration.

Rømmegrøt = traditional Norwegian porridge made from sour cream, milk, and flour. It's commonly served with raisins, cinnamon, and melted butter, and sometimes smoked or salted meats.

Sandnøtter = small, vanilla-flavored cookies primarily made from sugar and butter which makes them crumbly like sand. I made these the day before my son was born, and when nausea began, I blamed it on taste-testing the buttery dough a bit too much—in reality, I was just in early labor, and my all-time favorite Christmas present was born the next morning.

Selbuvott = traditional Norwegian mittens, from Selbu in Telemark, the tips of the mittens narrow to a point, and the geometrical pattern often centers around the eight-leafed rose.

Sirupssnipp = Norwegian Christmas cookie more similar to gingersnaps than pepperkaker. These cookies are diamond-shaped, cut with a squiggly cookie cutter wheel, and have one scalded, halved almond in the middle.

Smultringer = Norwegian fried dough, either made circular like doughnuts or folded in a knot.

Strømpepinner = five knitting needles used instead of circular needles to knit socks and mittens.

Vafler = traditional Norwegian everyday dessert, often shaped as a circle of five hearts joined in the middle. They are sweeter and softer than the Belgian style of waffles common in America.

CHAPTER 1

THORLEIF

December 9th

A nyone with a lick of sense would have stayed close to the *Jøtul* stove in the house—not beg fate for a frostbite in the bitter cold of an upstate New York winter. I frown at the blue-eyed girl who's the reason I lost that lick of sense the moment she walked through the door tonight. Or more accurately—since the day she walked through that door, clinging to her mom's skirts, nineteen years ago.

"He's the most handsome man I've ever met. And he's so kind! You should just see the way he treats the little kids that come in like a barrage on the weekends…." Ragnhild's lovestruck voice trails off, and her happy sigh floats into the winter night. Unfortunately for me, the guy she's been waxing poetic about for the last fifteen minutes isn't me.

We're standing at the top of the hill, right where the lane widens into the large field above my family's farm. Twilight seeps in from the woods surrounding us, and one by one the stars pop out into the dark sky.

We're too far out to be overheard by anyone crossing the farm yard—not that my mother or grandmother would even think about doing so in this cold. Nor would they have much reason. The goat barn has been empty for years, and I've stacked the firewood outside the door to the backroom so it's within easy reach from the house.

"He hasn't asked you out though, has he?" I don't know what her co-worker's deal is—Ragnhild is as gorgeous as they come.

My breath catches in my chest as she gazes back up at me with eyes bluer than a summer sky. And suddenly I really, really wish we were standing here alone for a different reason. But I swallow down that thought and listen to Ragnhild's answer.

"I think he hasn't worked up the courage yet." She shrugs and pushes a lock of red hair behind her ear. My gaze follows the motion. Her hair mimics spun bronze in the sun, but in the dwindling light in this frozen field it's just dark. "He spends all his shifts flirting with me, though."

"Is that what you lured me up here to talk about?" I shift my gaze away from the bundle of scarves that is the girl next to me and kick at an abandoned beer can courtesy of the neighboring farm kids. I glance at my boots balancing on the frozen mud tracks, then down the hill to my family's farm. But no matter how high I hunch my shoulders, the icy wind chills my skin as if my flannel shirt isn't even there.

Ragnhild touches my sleeve to get my attention. Little does she know she already has it—that she always does. Especially now when her touch burns through the thin fabric, straight to my skin.

"I need a favor from you." She gazes at me with earnest eyes I've never been able to turn down—oblivious as always to the way her nearness makes my pulse quicken. I'll do just about anything to make Ragnhild happy.

"I need to stage a wedding, and I need you to be the groom."

I still. My heart thunders in my chest, and blood pounds in my ears. Did she just say what I think she said? No, she couldn't have. It would make no sense in the light of the grueling minutes I've just spent listening to her awestruck monologue. I force a breath in through my nose, and with the biting winter air comes sense. She said *stage* a wedding—she's not proposing a real one. Lord knows I'd be all over that in a heartbeat.

I push down the disappointment raging in my chest. Still, now that my heart has slowed off just a bit, I can't help but give her a hard time. "You want me to marry you?"

Ragnhild's jaw drops, and she gapes at me. "No! Not for real! A *fake* wedding!" Does she have to look so horrified?

But I don't let that thought linger long. She's blushing furiously, and she's so cute it takes effort to hide my smile. Somehow I manage to keep it out of my voice. "Do you think maybe you read too many romance novels?"

I know for a fact that she reads too many romance novels. But she doesn't know that I know that, or that I'm aware of her secret stash of them behind the woodbox in the backroom of the farmhouse.

I glance longingly back down the hill to where the smoke rises from the chimney of the main house. I didn't grab my coat earlier, hoping this would be a quick walk to the field. But nothing is quick when it comes to the girl at my side. The girl whose gaze is still locked on me.

"So why do you need us to get married?"

"Fake married." The tips of her ears are still pink. "Because when he sees me about to get married, he'll realize what an idiot he's been and stop the wedding."

At least she's got the idiot part right, but the rest? "You want me to pretend to be your fiance so your coworker will ask you out?" There's no real reason to clarify what she's asked of me. It's quite simple—and impossible.

I don't think I've realized quite how deep my feelings run for

Ragnhild—not until this moment. The same moment in which this last plan of hers has made it quite clear that she's not interested in me. Not as anything other than a decoy groom, at least.

"I know it sounds crazy, but it will work! I'm sure of it!" Ragnhild's voice pulls me back to the present; back to facing my role in this ridiculous plan she's concocted.

I shake my head and push out a breath that is half laughter, half disbelief. That's my girl—always ready with a new hare-brained scheme to ease the sting of failure from the last. Except, she's not exactly my girl. And apparently, I need to hurry up if I want to change that.

"Will it work as well as your article about my ancestor trying to marry the king did?" I mumble the words under my breath.

Not quietly enough, I realize, when Ragnhild bristles next to me. She pulls far enough away that the icy December air has a chance to dance between our bodies. "Mentioning that particular ancestor and the king's tour in my article was a mistake. You know I never meant for it to go viral, or for my quotes to be used out of context. Hardly any of my other ideas have failed as spectacularly."

But pretty near all of them have. Ranghild's big heart and incorrigible impulsive streak get her into more scrapes than she can reasonably get out of. In fifth grade when she tried to reinvent ketchup with strawberry jam and spices; in high school when she decided to foster six kittens, leading to her apartment needing professional flea bombing. Accusing my grandmother's ancestor of modern-day gold-digging is far from her only flopped idea—and she knows that as well as I do. Does keeping my mouth shut right now make me a good friend or a bad one?

Ragnhild sets her shoulders and tosses her ponytail, feigning indifference that might have convinced someone who doesn't know her as well as I do. "Bestemor is speaking to you again, isn't she?"

I roll my eyes. Her casual comment doesn't reflect the rift between Ragnhild and Bestemor—nor the way Ragnhild sobbed into my shoulder when she realized the extent of it.

Ragnhild has wanted to be a writer since she learned to put letters together, so Bestemor agreed to let her use her as a source for an explorative piece on her Norwegian heritage. Published online, it swiftly went viral.

Ragnhild had been delirious with joy. Together we'd watched the comment section blow up, and she'd thrown her arms around me so exuberantly I honestly thought she'd kiss me right there and then. There'd been no kiss, then or later, but she'd walked on sunshine for about a week. Until we realized a few offhand sentences had turned the article into a salacious review of one female ancestor's attempt to snag the king touring the country for her husband—and that *that* was the reason it had made headlines. Bestemor hadn't appreciated it much.

"That she's speaking to me doesn't mean she's forgotten." My words come out a bit sterner than I intend, but seeing Bestemor so heartbroken pains me still, and I'm not so sure she's over it. And I'm certain Ragnhild and Bestemor's relationship hasn't returned to what it was six months ago—before the article went viral.

"I said I was sorry. You know I am!" Ragnhild's eyes blaze with anger—but the wrinkle forming at the top of her nose does nothing to intimidate me and everything to remind me of all the ways she affects me. It takes every bit of my restraint to keep from wrapping her up in my arms and kissing that wrinkle right off her nose.

I must have stepped closer, or maybe she did, because my face is suddenly inches from hers. Her warm, foggy breath fans my skin, and I can't help but shift my gaze from her glare to her full lips. Lips I wouldn't mind getting better acquainted with one bit.

But instead of closing the distance between us, Ragnhild steps back. Cold air replaces her warm breath, throwing a bucket of water over my desire. Right, because she only sees me as a brother—made all the clearer by her request.

Ragnhild clears her throat, eyes everywhere but on me. "All I need is for you to pretend we're getting married. I'll schedule the wedding at the Norwegian Seamen's Church on a day when Jacob is working, and he'll realize he'll have to *speak now or forever hold his peace.*"

I roll my eyes. The guy is a dud if he needs any sort of motivation to notice a girl like Ragnhild. Especially considering all the nights she's spent in the staff apartments to avoid the commute since her internship started. Her co-worker has had his chance.

But instead of telling her that, I straighten to my full height and shove down the disappointment in my chest. Ragnhild and I have been best friends since the summer her mother decided to try her luck as an actress, leaving her preschool daughter in the care of the neighbors—which happened to be my family.

Clearly, I've gained little ground in the two decades we've spent together compared to this guy she's staging a wedding to hook. I try to catch her eyes again, but everything in our frozen surroundings seems to fascinate her to no end.

I sigh. I probably shouldn't have looked so much like I wanted to kiss her.

Why did I look so much like I wanted to kiss her?

Because I do. I really want to kiss her.

"So will you help me, or what?" Her gaze shoots quickly to mine —long enough to pose the question, but not long enough for me to have time to make cow eyes at her. As if I would.

I clear my throat and shove both hands into the pockets of my stiff, cold jeans. "I will help you, but just for the record: I don't think it's a good idea. And if Bestemor gets hurt again—"

"You'll leave me stranded on the side of the highway and never talk to me again. I get it." The words rush out as if she's worried I'll change my mind if she doesn't immediately agree to all my terms.

A smile tilts the corner of my lips. There's not much chance of me leaving her stranded anywhere—regardless of what she does. But I'm not certain she knows that. Just like she doesn't know that she's *it* for me. She's been my partner in crime for as long as I can remember, with her ridiculous ideas, determined optimism, and killer sense of humor. I can't imagine anyone taking her place.

But Ragnhild doesn't see my fond smile. Her gaze lingers a few feet away, on the beer can I knocked into the brush—a glaringly obvious excuse to avoid meeting my eyes.

I pull in a deep breath and take in the girl who's been next to me all my life. And yet she has never stirred me quite like she does now. Maybe if I give her time, she'll one day return my feelings. Will she notice if I sneak a higher ratio of best-friends-to-lovers romances into her secret stockpile? And if she does, will she just think my mother is trying to speed things along?

I'll need to give the idea more thought when I'm out of these frigid temps. I can practically feel my brain cells wither and die with each lungful of frozen air. Or maybe that's just Ragnhild's presence. "Okay, let's head out. I need to be up early."

Ragnhild turns from her study of the half-crushed metal cylinder and nods. She shoots me a small smile and takes the lead down the hill towards the houses. I keep my eyes firmly trained on the swinging ponytail sticking out from her bundled form, and far away from the sway of her hips.

I want to look, of course I do, but I know she'd put my head on a spike if she ever caught me checking her out. And so out of respect for her, and because I rather enjoy my head attached to my body, I don't. Except that I can't just look the other way and pretend I don't see her. Not when I'm somehow supposed to pose as the fake groom of a woman I'm wildly attracted to; a woman I'd like to marry for real.

Ragnhild's latest idea might be even wilder than her article about my devious ancestors, and it took nothing but a doe-eyed gaze from her to make me sign up for the madness right alongside her.

What on earth have I gotten myself into?

CHAPTER 2

RAGNHILD

The chill magnifies each scuffle of our boots against the frozen ground. I might have started out ahead on the narrow path down from the field, but the moment the trail widens Thorleif trudges up to walk by my side.

I don't mind—he's a giant and as such he's a nice shield from the bitter wind. He also makes me feel a million times safer walking through the dark. The howls of a band of coyotes sound in the distance, and the yapping wails chill me to my soul.

I tuck imperceptibly closer to the massive man next to me. I know coyotes are unlikely to attack me right here on the footpath, but I have a vivid imagination—and in the darkness, it does me no favors. I'm fairly certain Thorleif could easily fight off a coyote, though. And I know he would, for me.

The thick tension between us in the field tonight doesn't change that. Our friendship is way too old—too solid. Even that almost kiss won't change it. My stomach tightens. Was that what that was? Did my best friend almost kiss me?

My cheeks heat despite the punishing cold, and I push the thought away. Of course, he didn't. We're just…not kids anymore. Isn't…. Isn't there bound to be some tension between friends of the opposite sex? That's all this is. Normal sexual tension between two adults who have both been single for a long time. Now that I think about it, has Thorleif even had a girlfriend in recent years?

I bite down on my lower lip and wrack my brain for a girl who lasted more than two dates. Nothing. I could ask Thorleif, of course, but he's being his normal broody self, doing that ancestral Viking thing where he looks absolutely murderous despite just being deep in thought—not in fact planning a raid on an unsuspecting English monastery.

Not that Thorleif's quiet presence intimidates me. I know him well enough to know that even if I rejected a thousand of his kisses he'd still protect me from any danger pouncing from the dark woods on either side of the trail. There are many threats in these woods. The coyotes are shy, and unlikely to come near. Then there are the bears, which are mostly the same. A chill trails my spine. Just knowing there are bears in this area is enough to make me stay inside after dark for the rest of my life. Unfortunately, this desire hasn't been compatible with being a working adult.

The buildings of the farm come into view—the wagon shed, the tiny pig barn, and the garage—and I let my shoulders sink a little. As safe as I feel with Thorleif's large presence next to me, I miss the easy humor that usually accompanies us on walks like these.

I miss the corners of his eyes crinkling when he thinks I'm funny but doesn't want me to know. The glint of mischief deep in his dark eyes, and the quiet humor tugging at his mouth. I'm funny, and he knows it. I've heard him repeat my jokes to his mother and grand-mother, and their howls of laughter confirmed it.

The cold, clear night makes my nose burn. I push my scarf up to cover it, suddenly feeling a pinch of remorse for pulling Thorleif out here. I glance over at my best friend in the world, at his hunched shoulders and the large hands he's jammed into his pockets. He's been outside this whole time in nothing but his shirt—he has to be absolutely freezing.

I didn't mean for him to freeze. I just needed to talk to him alone, and the centuries-old farmhouse he calls home wasn't built for privacy. It makes my plan seem so illicit when we can only talk of it in the field. But I have no choice. I can't risk Mor Vaage or Bestemor overhearing. Goodness knows what might be set in motion if either of the Vaage women catches the word "marriage" in a conversation between Thorleif and me.

I shudder.

"Are you cold?" This from the man wearing jeans and a flannel shirt outside in single-digit weather. The man who'll still give me that shirt off his back if he thinks I need it. Not because of any romantic feelings, or even in a show of chivalry, but because that's who Thorleif is.

Warmth spreads in my chest at his concern, but I shake my head. "I'm not cold. Just...thinking."

Thorleif grunts, but he doesn't ask what I was thinking. He never does—ever content to wait until I eventually spill my guts after another late night of coffee and talking. *I'm* the friend who will stop at nothing to get to the bottom of his feelings. Well, except for whatever that was in the field earlier. I absolutely do not want to know what was behind his intense gaze as he leaned towards me. My pulse gets a little erratic just thinking about it.

I'm certain both Mor Vaage and Bestemor, avid romance readers as they are, have considered a match between us hundreds of times already. There'd be nothing but ecstatic responses if either of us ever announced romantic intentions towards the other. At any point in time.

Except perhaps for a while after my article went viral. I feel sick when I remember the betrayal on Bestemor's face when she returned from the senior center. She did me a generous favor when she sat down to explain her lineage, and I repaid her by accidentally painting her foremothers as gold diggers with a one-track mind. And somehow every single one of her girlfriends at the senior center read it. Which might be a bigger miracle than the internet itself. And while I've gotten myself into plenty of scrapes through the years, I've never wanted anyone's forgiveness as badly as I do hers.

I glance back over at Bestemor's oldest grandson, and his eyes catch mine. The passion from his earlier speech still burns in the depths of his eyes, and butterflies spring to life in my stomach. His brown hair wild and full beard covering his jaw, Thorleif looks back at me with all the fire and steadfastness of his Viking forefathers—and the effect is stunning.

For a moment I can't breathe—my lungs as caught up in the singular attention of this man as I am. Walking seemed so easy just a second ago, but with his eyes on me putting my feet down correctly is a struggle. Even more so when my brain replays the moment when his gaze shifted to my lips in the field earlier.

Then the vanishing inches between us that made my mouth go dry. Then and now.

Another delicious shiver trails my spine.

Just normal sexual tension between adults! It's normal. And if I wasn't worried he'd stumble across my search history, I'd Google it to make sure.

But regardless of what I call this tension, he was about to kiss me —I'm certain of that now. As certain as I am that I need to step back and remind myself that Thorleif is like a brother to me. This weird reaction I'm having to him has nothing to do with any romantic feelings. And it's definitely not why I asked him to be my groom. My *very fake* groom.

Thorleif has been my best friend since we were kids, and I need his help. That's all. I can't let his sudden attraction derail me from my plan to make Jacob finally realize what a perfect match we'd make. Jacob, who is without a doubt, the hottest guy I've ever laid eyes on. Who helps out at the downtown soup kitchen every Thursday. Who never refuses to help anyone who crosses his path, young or old.

The long days of slaving away in the hot kitchens over steaming waffle irons to feed the hundreds of guests visiting the church on weekends have only been worth it because it meant time spent with him. It's even been worth the scent of butter and cardamom lingering on my hair and skin long after my shower.

Just the thought of Jacob's flash of teeth at the end of a long shift warms my insides. Tingles run up my spine as I remember the brush of his hand when he handed me a stack of papers last week. And that conversation we had about his soup kitchen work? My heartbeat quickens.

"Ragnhild? Please keep my family out of it this time." Is that exasperation in his voice?

"I will. I promise." I meet his gaze, and my brain chooses that moment to replay the moment in the field again—and my heart trembles. The emotion that flitted across his face as he straightened…. Was it disappointment? Annoyance? Would he have kissed me if I'd stayed in place? If I'd waited for him another second?

But his frown only digs deeper between his brows as he watches me until I can't stand the intensity of his gaze any longer and drop mine to my boots. "There's no need to threaten me with bodily harm if I hurt your family's feelings again. I love your family as much as my own."

His boot taps mine playfully, and I look back up at him. He dips his head and lets out a long sigh. "I know that, Ragnhild."

I chew on my lip inside my scarf, searching his familiar face. "Do you really?"

Is he just appeasing me? I know the lengths this man will go to to please me. That is, after all, why I've asked him to marry me.

To *pretend* to marry me. The word "pretend" is very important in this situation.

Thorleif dips his chin, and in the dim light from the lantern mounted on the goat barn, I read sincerity in his eyes. We start walking again and pass the woodshed. A few more steps and the soles of our boots move from the dead grass onto the gravel at the top of the driveway where my car is parked.

Thorleif stops in the middle of the yard, my car on one side, his house on the other. He shifts, and the searing porch light clicks on.

How many times have the two of us tried to hold still long enough to make the motion sensor light turn off? Or taken bets on how long we'd be able to talk in the dark without setting it off again? How many times has my habit of talking with my hands lost me that bet?

It's been our game for years. But the Thorleif so sharply outlined in the porch light doesn't look like he wants to play. Half in shadow, half in the stark, pale light, he's intimidating—again bringing the ferocity of his Nordic ancestors to mind.

Thorleif rests his fists on his hips. His chest rises, then falls as he lets the deep breath back out with an even deeper sigh. His eyes move to mine. What is he thinking? His stony features reveal nothing, neither does his voice when he speaks. "So Saturday the twenty-first?"

Will he pretend to marry me on that Saturday? Yes. "Saturday the twenty-first."

It's my turn to shove my hands into my jacket pockets. But I immediately pull them back out and step forward. Thorleif's strong, calloused fingers wrap around mine—one squeeze, and he lets go. It's the most innocent of touches. It shouldn't make my stomach drop, should it?

I hurry to my car. Once inside, I don't pause like I normally would, but immediately back down the driveway. My thoughts are a whirling mess as I drive home. Thorleif has held my hand so many times over the years—for so many reasons. Why does it suddenly feel so different? Since when does his palm feel so much larger than mine?

Has his skin against mine ever sent jolts of lightning up my arm before? And if it hasn't, why on earth should it start now? And more importantly, how do I make it stop so that our relationship can go back to the way it was before?

CHAPTER 3

THORLEIF

The bells on the backdoor jingle as I shut the door behind me. Kicking off my boots, I place them on the rug my mother keeps by the door for that very reason. I push aside the hanging blanket separating the open porch from the living room where the little black *Jøtul* stove keeps these frosty winter nights at bay.

I step into the welcoming heat, rubbing my frozen palms together. My mother looks up from the newspaper she's reading. "Ragnhild isn't staying for supper?"

The way she peeled out of the driveway, that much was obvious. But I don't point that out since my mother didn't. Instead, I shake my head, run my hands up and down my frozen biceps to get the blood pumping, and step close to the singeing heat of the wood stove. "She'd already eaten."

It's late for supper, but since Ragnhild accosted me with her idea right as I got home from work, I haven't had mine yet. The pleading in her eyes wasn't something I could resist on an empty stomach.

My mother's kind eyes, almost as blue as Ragnhild's, look me over, much like they did when I was younger. Back then she sought scuffs and scrapes of the physical kind. These days her eyes seem to search deeper than the surface, never missing anything. Even something as slight as the bruises on my heart. And there have been a few of those lately. "Did you have a good talk?"

I grunt. Good talk? Sure, but I'd have preferred a different type of talk. One with fewer words, and more.... Well, things I've never had with Ragnhild. Things that seem less and less likely that I'll ever have with her—and yet, I can't help hoping. Hoping that she'll suddenly see reason and ask me up to the field for a very different conversation. One that would end in an actual kiss and not just her frantic avoidance of my gaze.

And I'm a fool, because I still hope for this. Even as she's literally asked me to pretend to be in a relationship with her so she can catch some stupid city boy's attention.

My mother's attention stays on me even though her eyes are back on the newspaper. Sometimes I think she knows about my feelings for Ragnhild, at other times I'm not so sure. She's never said anything about it to me. Though how could she miss it? My mother doesn't miss much, and she's seen us together since we were little. How would she not notice that something is different between us now?

I leave my mother to her paper and walk into the kitchen. The tang of baked goods floats in the air—as if the scent of cardamom is baked into the very walls. Taking in a deep breath, I let my shoulders settle. The gas burner clicks as I turn it on and move the kettle onto it. Then I drop four scoops of coffee into the small French press.

Ragnhild might be frustrating me to no end, but I suppose even unrequited love isn't enough of a tragedy that it can't be fixed with a cup of coffee. I grin at the thought of sharing my sentiment with my mother. I'm certain she'd fully agree. Norwegians love their coffee—everyone in this household drinks several cups a day. So many, in fact, that we really should invest in a coffee maker. But when it comes down to it, I think we all like the taste of French-pressed coffee too much.

I turn from the coffee and spot a tea towel covering up something lumpy. Hope rises in my chest. Did my mother make a kringle? I cross the kitchen and lift the edge of the cloth.

Jackpot.

The thick rope of cardamom flavored sweet dough, juicy raisins, and succades calls to me—evoking memories of sitting on Bestemor's lap gobbling up a large piece of freshly glazed kringle, still warm from the oven. I swallow, knowing I'll have to find a way to get a piece of this.

Just as I reach out my hand, my mother's voice rings out from the other room. "Thorleif! It's not even glazed yet. Let it cool."

I grin and stretch my neck to see her still in her rocking chair next to the small stove, her back towards me. What is that saying about mothers having eyes in the backs of their heads? Clearly, it's no myth when it comes to mine.

"Just one piece, *vær så snill?*" I know she'll soften at my use of the Norwegian phrase for "please".

"Just the one." The words are accompanied by a deep sigh, but I know she would be worried if I one day didn't beg for the first piece of her irresistible baked goods. I reach for the knife block, and knife in hand, I turn towards the fresh pastry.

"An edge piece, please." My mother's direction from the other room doesn't make things any clearer.

I frown at the pretzel-shaped loaf. "How do I find the edge? It's round?" I will never understand this.

I sense her shrug from the living room. "Just somewhere it will look inconspicuous."

It's my turn to sigh deeply, but I do as she says—or I make an honest attempt at doing what she says. I leave "inconspicuous" up to my personal judgment and slice a piece off from the bottom of the kringle. Then I search the countertop for the glaze.

"In the fridge."

I grin wider at my mother's continued ability to anticipate my every move from the living room. When I find the glaze in the fridge, I drizzle it over my plated piece of kringle, mouth watering in anticipation.

The first bite is heaven—as is the second. I suck the powdered-sugar glaze off my thumb. When I open my mouth for a third bite, the kettle whistles behind me.

I pour the hot water into the French press as my thoughts venture back to the redhead who trailed behind me up to the field—just as she's done for most of my life. For the longest time, my strides were too long for her short legs, and she'd hold my hand, dragging behind me. Eventually, her legs grew, and she caught up.

A smile tugs my lips at the memory. I was five, and she was a four-year-old with a penchant for swiping my treats once she finished her own—Ragnhild has never been above sneaking rice crispy bars right out of a man's pants pockets. And her pout had been cute enough I let her. It still is, judging by my agreeing to her ridiculous plan.

We've been inseparable ever since we were kids, but I've never given Ragnhild much thought when she wasn't around. I noticed her when she got older, of course. When she turned fifteen and I was sixteen, I definitely paid attention.

I bite into my kringle piece and grab a coffee mug from the dish drainer.

I had a bit of a crush on fifteen-year-old Ragnhild. She never returned it, of course, and eventually, I went back to thinking about her only when she was in view. But these days? These days, she's no longer fifteen, but a full-grown woman. And I can no longer get her out of my head.

I pour the hot coffee and move my attention to the counter where the kringle is hidden under a tea towel. Do I dare?

"Thorleif Vaage, I said one piece!"

A grin splits my face, and coffee cup in hand I amble out to the living room to kiss the top of my mother's head. *"Ja, mor."* Yes, mother.

She narrows her eyes at me, but I see the smile lurking in the blue depths. I drop down on the couch with my kringle piece and cup of coffee. My mother curls her fingers around her coffee cup and lifts it to her lips. Then she pushes back a strand of hair escaping her hair clip. The color of that hair is a perfect match to mine, though it looks darker with the silver strands threading it now.

The living room is quiet and cozy; the only sounds are the flutter of newspaper pages and the intermittent snaps and crackles of the fire. The clicking sound of Bestemor's knitting needles and the creaking of her rocking chair, though, are strangely absent. "Where's Bestemor?"

My mother flips over another page of her newspaper. "In her room."

There's no sign of the small frown that appears between her brows when she's worried, but my shoulders still tense. I put down my coffee. "Is she alright?"

Bestemor hasn't been herself since Ragnhild's article sparked a stir at the senior center lunch this summer. She's also since been noticeably absent whenever Ragnhild is around. Not that I can blame her. It took quite a while for the extra attention to die down. Apparently, it had been a while since the senior center had had such juicy gossip.

I hate that what should have been a victory for Ragnhild's writing career still sits like a wall between two of the most important people in my life.

But no signs of worry are visible on my mother's face. She pushes off from the wood floor with her slippered foot, and her rocking chair creaks just a little. Time for another round of WD-40 on those hinges. "I think she might be working on Christmas presents."

The tension in my shoulders eases a little, and I lift my coffee mug to my mouth. "I suppose it is the time for that."

My mother rocks back and forth with her new momentum, but at my words, she lets out a silvery laugh. Her dancing eyes catch mine. "Yes, it's actually high time if you plan to knit anything bigger than a washcloth. Christmas is fourteen days away, Thorleif."

I roll my eyes at the expectation on her face. "Thankfully, I don't have any knitting projects on my gift list." I barely have a gift list.

Though if I'm being honest, there's a girl I'd like to give something small and shiny—but seeing as she just recruited me for a fake wedding, I don't think the time is right for that.

What would my mother say if I told her Ragnhild and I were faking a relationship? I'm certain she wouldn't approve, but would that be because she'd want it to be real? Not that it matters much as that option isn't even on the table.

Nerves tighten my stomach as I go over Ragnhild's crazy plan in my mind again. Is she really so clueless about how I feel about her? But she must be—why else would she ask me to pose as her groom in her wedding farce?

The way she avoided my eyes makes me think she isn't as clueless as her words would make it appear. But if she knows how I feel she has to know that there's no way this fake relationship will be anything but a disaster.

I groan, quickly covering my face with my tilted coffee mug when my mother shoots me a questioning glance.

How long does Ragnhild expect me to fake being in a relationship with her? What does she expect me to do? Will I even make it all the way to the ceremony without letting my true intentions slip?

CHAPTER 4

RAGNHILD

December 12th

The subway is as packed as always, and I'd be lying if I didn't say that just entering it makes my skin crawl. The stuffy heat is no relief from the freezing temperatures that have pummeled the state in the last week; not when it's accompanied by the body odor and coffee breath of a crowd of strangers.

If there's one thing I've learned on my weekly trips to the city since October it's this; I do not enjoy commuting. I don't even think I enjoy the city as much as I thought I would. It's much filthier in person, and the stressed-out people in this place are either miserable beyond belief or downright mean. Or perhaps it's a cause-and-effect kind of thing.

Thank goodness this is only for the fall semester. The extra money has been good, and the college credits I'm receiving simply for the internship are, too. But in reality, there's only one reason I haven't absolutely hated these last few months—and he flashed me a sexy grin when he left the Norwegian Seamen's Church an hour ago.

A soft sigh slips across my lips as I ponder my co-worker. Jacob is fun and flirty; just a year or so older than me. And the once-over he gave me this morning makes me blush even now, squeezed in between strangers in the least romantic space on earth. And it made the hour I agonized over my outfit last night very worth it.

It's not rare for me to develop a lightning-speed crush on a guy. Even Thorleif will admit I'm a hopeless romantic, and he doesn't even know about my voracious romance reading habit. What is rare is to have a guy return my interest. And I'm certain Jacob likes me, too. He works in accounting, so I don't see him much. But when I do?

I push out a breath, just barely resisting the urge to fan myself.

When we unexpectedly ran into each other in the hallway this morning, the glint in his eyes was downright wolfish. Add that to the fact that he's volunteered four out of the five weekends I've been scheduled for waffle duty, and his interest is clear. He certainly doesn't sign up because he loves the way the buttery cardamom scent lingers on our clothes even after washing.

Jacob is the real deal. And he is so, so good. How often do you find a single guy who is handsome, good with kids, *and* volunteers weekly at the soup kitchen downtown? What is a girl supposed to do when said guy starts flirting with her? Fall madly in love, that's what.

The only thing Jacob hasn't done is pull me into an empty office to kiss me or ask me out on a date. But he's hinted—he's definitely hinted. And since my contract will only keep me here through the holiday season, I'll be gone by the end of December. Which is why I need him to move a bit faster.

I hope to God I can pull off this fake wedding ceremony. I already hate myself for putting Thorleif through it, but I have no choice. Not with Christmas less than two weeks away.

I spend the next four hours driving through the dreary white and brown upstate New York landscape, alternating between daydreaming about Jacob and paying attention to my latest sizzling office romance streaming through my earbuds. When I finally pull into the parking spot in front of a two-story house that's seen better days, my lower back feels like it's made from granite. I rub it gently as I trudge up the creaky stairs to the second-floor apartment I call mine, and shove the key into the lock.

Thank goodness I'm not repeating that drive for another couple of days. Plus, the break will give me time to cram for my finals. Studying for my bachelor's degree online might allow me to live in the middle of nowhere, but I still have to study on the days when I'm not interning in the big city. And I have a lot of studying to catch up on.

But first, I'll need to eat.

I'm staring at the two measly packs of ramen noodles and a single can of green beans in my paint-chipped cupboard when my phone dings. I fish it out of my back pocket, and a smile immediately stretches my cheeks when I see whose number is flashing on my screen.

Thorleif: Sure you want ramen tonight?

Me: Are you spying on me?

Thorleif: No. I figured you'd be home by now. And also staring into your dismal cupboards.

I roll my eyes, because he knows me too well. I lean against the kitchen counter as I type out a response.

Me: Are you just rubbing it in, or are you offering solutions?

Thorleif: I'm on my way home from Olav's, thought I'd stop by.

The dots at the bottom of the screen keep moving, and I wait for his justification. Thorleif's mode of operation is to be as premeditated as I am impulsive. His attention to detail has probably kept me out of a fair share of trouble over the years, so I know for a fact he'll have a good excuse to stop by.

Thorleif: With a sub I picked up on the way?

Me: I love you.

The bubbles start moving. Then they stop. They start moving again.

A niggle of unease stirs in my gut. Maybe I shouldn't have typed that. Not after that weird tension between us in the field three nights ago. When he tried to kiss me. Why did I type that? What if he takes my declaration of love the wrong way?

I press two fingers against the tension wrinkle forming between my eyebrows. A week ago I would have sent off that text without a second thought; my statement was pure impulse. But now, with last night's sexual tension still in the air between us? Maybe I need to hold back a bit. But then his text pings through. I scan the words, and my shoulders relax, relief coursing through my bloodstream.

Thorleif: Are you talking to me or the sub?

Me: The sub.

Thorleif: Thought so.

Twenty minutes later, there are heavy footfalls on the stairs and a knock at my door.

"It's unlocked!"

Thorleif pushes open the front door, and in the next moment, he seems to fill my entire apartment. He's still in his work boots, worn jeans, and a green flannel shirt. His style is so quintessentially redneck that it's hard to believe that he was raised by a strong Norwegian woman—with equally strong, Nordic ideas about equality between the sexes. Mor Vaage has never allowed her son to treat me like less than him, or expect me to be any more domestic than him just because I'm a girl. And I not so secretly love her for it. It may also be the reason he's my best friend. Something tells me misogyny wouldn't be an asset in our relationship.

"Hey." Thorleif the redneck-imposter tosses two large, thin cardboard boxes on the counter next to me. When I spot the cartoonish illustration of Santa and his reindeer across them, I gasp. "You got us chocolate advent calendars?"

I know I'm way too old to be this excited about twenty-four

minuscule pieces of cheap German chocolate, but I can't help it. These calendars were a staple of childhood at the Vaage house—the only semblance of childhood I had.

And Thorleif knows.

Warmth unfurls in my chest as I gaze up at him. His image blurs, and I blink the tears away. "Thank you! How did you know I was kicking myself for not picking one up earlier in the month? I haven't seen them anywhere since the first week of December!"

He grins. "I didn't know that. But you seemed like you'd had a rough day and needed a pick-me-up."

I frown. "You haven't seen me today."

He digs a paper-wrapped sub sandwich out of a bag and pushes my cereal bowl from Saturday morning away so he can put the sandwich on the counter. "You just texted me."

"You got that from our texts?" I lift my phone and scroll through our last conversation. "How on earth did you get that from any of the texts I sent you?" He's either a mind-reader, or he knows me better than I know myself.

"You seemed down." He shrugs as if my prodding is making him uncomfortable. But this isn't the little thing he tries to pretend it is —he went out of his way to get me something he knew would cheer me up. Who cares that he only spent a couple of dollars on these? Emotionally, they're worth a crisp hundred-dollar bill.

"Thank you, Thorleif."

He nods in acknowledgment, but under the dark scruff, his neck is a little red. He rubs a calloused hand over the back of his neck. "So, are you going to eat this?"

I grin at his embarrassment, because somehow it makes his thoughtfulness even sweeter. I guess I can let him off the hook, though, just for today. "Movie?"

He dips his head. "Sure! As long as it's not another sappy, romantic—"

"Thorleif." I roll my eyes, because as wonderful as this man is, he needs to learn to read the room. "It's December, what else would we watch other than a Hallmark movie?"

He groans, but he knew this was coming. With a look of utter defeat, he grabs the sub and napkins and drops down on the couch. It's not a studio apartment, but it's pretty tiny. There aren't many steps from the kitchen counter to the couch I picked up from the curbside one town over.

I drop down next to him, fully intent on torturing him with the sappiest, most romantic Hallmark Christmas movie I can find. But every preview I scan brings back the memory of our crackling chemistry in that field, and I suddenly realize that I cannot watch anything with a kissing scene right now. Not even a standard Hall-mark press-mouths-together-and-hold-for-three-seconds-kiss. Not alone with Thorleif—not after he leaned in to kiss me.

We settle on some weird British Christmas movie where a single dad inherits a farm in the countryside. An unhinged farmhand secretly lives in his barn, and the small town surrounding the farm is all up in his business. But there's no kissing, and it's a cute movie. Out of the corner of my eye, I catch Thorleif's mouth twitching in his beard, so he obviously also finds it entertaining.

As soon as he's swallowed the last bite of his sub, Thorleif jumps up from the couch.

I startle, still only halfway through my meal, and already caught up in the storyline of the movie. "Where are you going?"

He doesn't even turn around but goes straight for the still-messy kitchen counter. "Calendars."

I gasp, hand against my heart, while employing my best pearl-clutching voice. "You can't possibly be thinking about desecrating the spirit of Christmas by opening the chocolate calendars out of turn?"

He grins as he turns around, shaking the calendars till the chocolate pieces inside them rattle. "We're twelve days into the month, remember? There are twelve chocolates in here to be devoured without desecrating anything. Twenty-four between the two of us."

I gasp, because I'd honestly forgotten the significance of getting the calendars after December 1st. When Thorleif holds out a calendar to me, I snatch it with all the patience of a chocolate-deprived four-year-old. Which isn't very far from the truth.

Thorleif laughs at me, and I catch the glint of pleasure in his eyes. Suddenly I feel the old camaraderie between us reemerge. Warmth curls around my heart.

It's not gone.

Our friendship is still here, alive and intact.

Thorleif is still my best friend. Still the one person I'd pick to be my partner for any challenge. And even our weird attraction earlier this week hasn't eliminated it.

I stuff a candle-shaped piece of German chocolate in my mouth and breathe a sigh of relief.

CHAPTER 5

THORLEIF

December 13th, Luciadagen (St. Lucia Day)

Friday night, there's almost no work to do in the shop, so I get off work early enough to eat dinner with Bestemor and my mother. It's always a bit like a blast from the past—from back when it was just the three of us.

My mother and Bestemor still observe St. Lucia Day as if we were all back in the country where they spent their childhoods. When we were younger, Ragnhild and I would dress up in white robes in the predawn hours. We'd go singing to our neighbors, carrying burning candles and baskets of fresh saffron rolls, *lussekatter*.

It's been a few years since we celebrated it quite like that. Neither Ragnhild's nor my work schedule allows pre-dawn baking or strolls to the neighbors anymore. These days, instead of setting the dough the night before and baking it early, my mother sets it in the mornings, and we roll it out at night.

Ragnhild, even though she no longer relies on us to take care of her during her mother's long absences, still participates in the traditions we did as children. And tradition true, she'll be here later tonight to bake *lussekatter* with me and decorate them with raisins—adding too many so that the majority falls off and roasts in the oven. For reasons known only to herself, the girl I love finds burned raisins downright irresistible. Oh, to be a burnt raisin.

Those baking plans are the reason I walk through the door to a house that smells like rising bread dough, and to Bestemor humming the Lucia tune from her chair where she is working on a pair of mittens. Her cropped silver hair frames her face as she turns to smile at me.

My mother sits in her rocking chair reading her newspaper, but she glances up when I walk in. Just like she always has. And her smile has the same effect on me as it did when I was a child. There are few things as invigorating as my mother's smile when I walk into a room.

Well, perhaps there's one other smile.

That of the blue-eyed beauty currently studying for her finals at her second-floor apartment. I wish she was here for dinner as well, but she said she was eating with Ingrid tonight. Is she avoiding me, or does she just need to study that badly?

I can't shake the feeling that something about our relationship has changed since that night in the field. And not just because she asked me to pretend-marry her, or because I barely restrained myself from kissing her. Something deeper than that. There's a new awareness I don't remember from before.

"How was work?" My mother watches me intently, and for a second I wonder if I said the part about Ragnhild out loud. But no, there's no way I did.

Still, the blush creeps over my neck, and I rub a hand across my heated skin to ease the sensation. "Hard and draining, but I'm up and not crying."

A smile spills across her face, crinkling her eyes at the corners. The Norwegian saying is not one of hers, but when Olav's father,

her brother, was around, he used to say it quite a bit. "I'm glad you're home, Thorleif."

I cross the distance between us and drop a kiss onto her hair. "I'm glad you're home, too."

The second kiss goes to Bestemor, who pats my cheek in the way only she gets away with. "It's good to have you home." Her dark eyes are full of love, and I don't know how I got so lucky—to have the love and support of these two women in my life.

I leave my mother and Bestemor in the living room and make my way into the kitchen. Once there, I give my full attention to browning the ground beef and opening the can of crushed tomatoes. A couple of dashes of salt, pepper, sugar, and oregano later, and the meat sauce is simmering on the back burner.

My fingers are itching to text Ragnhild, but I'm trying to give her space. But is space what she wants? She usually texts me when she knows I'm done with work, but tonight she hasn't. Is that intentional?

Two tablespoons of butter sizzle in the pan.

Maybe she's studying. Maybe Ingrid is keeping her busy.

I stir in the flour and watch the melted butter turn into lumps.

Maybe I need to read less into the fact that the Hallmark movie she decided to torture me with last night didn't include as much as a romantic subplot—much less any actual romance. In fact, she skipped over every single movie with any hint of romance in the preview.

Milk, salt, pepper, and nutmeg go in while I stir.

The movie was funny and sweet, but usually sappy romance is Ragnhild's mojo. Was she worried she'd give me the wrong impression if we watched a romantic movie after the other night in the field? Or am I imagining her skittishness?

The sauce thickens, and I turn the burner off. My phone pings in my back pocket, and I very nearly strain a tendon trying to get to it with the speed of light.

As Ragnhild's name pops up on my screen, I decide it's probably worth the injury. I rub my sore arm and click to open the message.

Ragnhild: We're still baking later, right?

Nerves settle in my stomach. Is she trying to cancel on me?

Me: I'm going to pretend you didn't ask that. Is all the studying making your brain soft?

Ragnhild: I think some of it leaked out my left ear when I fell asleep on top of my keyboard. What time?

She's still coming. I push out a breath of relief.

Me: 7 pm. I'm still cooking.

Ragnhild: Send my condolences to your family.

I roll my eyes, because I'm probably a better cook than she is. But I still grate the cheese with a stupid grin on my face. The grin remains as I layer bechamel sauce, meat sauce, cheese, and lasagna noodles into a pan and stick it in the oven.

Another beep from the counter, and I wipe my hands on a towel and reach for the phone.

Ragnhild: Who else will be there? Can I bring Ingrid?

I frown as I type out my next response. Is this another attempt at keeping a buffer between us? Although I was expecting Olav to show up, maybe she wasn't. Is that why she's trying to invite Ingrid?

Me: Olav might show up. Bring Ingrid.

I don't mind the company at all, but I miss hanging out when it's just Ragnhild and me. Which seems like an exaggeration since we did hang out just the two of us less than twenty-four hours ago. Even if we did watch a movie without any hint of our normal sappy entertainment diet, though maybe that was actually an improvement.

I set the table while the lasagna cooks, then I dump down on the couch in the living room, and pick up my book from the coffee table. I crack open the pages, but I can barely focus on what I read. The more I think about it, the more likely it seems that Ragnhild really is attempting to avoid me. Probably because I almost kissed her.

But is her avoiding me a good thing or a bad thing in this situation? Does it mean she has feelings for me, too? Or the opposite?

"Is your book that terrible?"

"What?" I glance up at the sound of Bestemor's voice. Her smile is knowing, as if she can tell how frustrated I am over Ragnhild's avoidance. But surely she can't know that, can she?

"You're scowling."

I relax my facial muscles to revert from what Ragnhild calls my *resting murderous Viking face*. "The book is fine." I shrug and pretend I have any idea what's been happening over the last several pages.

Bestemor nods, but the twinkle in her eye is still there as she glances back down at the *Selbu* mitten she's knitting. She tugs another couple of inches of strings from the four balls of yarn in her lap. Just watching her keep it all straight makes me dizzy. She tried to teach me to knit with five needles when I was younger. *Strømpepinner*, she calls them. But, afraid I'd poke my eyes out, I didn't last more than a couple of lessons. I can knit, mind you. But I'm sticking to solid-colored scarves and the occasional set of circular needles for hats.

I knit Ragnhild a hat for Christmas when we were kids. I haven't seen it since. For all I know, she doesn't even own it anymore. I wouldn't blame her. I know I was dropping stitches like it was going out of style over the weeks of painstaking effort I spent making it.

And now I'm grinning, and sneaking a glance over at the rocking chair confirms what I already know—that Bestemor is watching, and probably judging, my mood swings.

I close my book and drop it to the table. There's no use in pretending, and from the smell of the lasagna that's starting to permeate the air, we'll soon have to eat supper anyways.

My mother lights two of the purple candles in the advent wreath on the table, while the three of us sing the verses that accompany them. My contribution is half-hearted. But then my heart is in a completely different place than the farmhouse living room where I've spent every night for as long as I can remember. My heart is in a dingy second-floor apartment that was redone decades before I was born, stubbornly residing with a feisty redhead probably still studying next to her bowl of ramen noodles.

After dinner, my mother does the dishes while I get started on the tray of gingersnap hearts the size of my palm. They're already threaded with red ribbon, and there are tiny nails above each downstairs window to hang them on. I place each gingersnap heart in the middle of each window, in the living room, kitchen, the backroom. Last I get to the back porch, and by the time all twelve are hanging in the windows, a car is pulling up the driveway.

My heart does a weird thud against my ribcage before I realize it's Olav's car and not Ragnhild's. He parks at the top of the driveway, jumps out, and makes it over to the house at record speed. Probably because he's wearing no more than a long-sleeved T-shirt, and the temperature is easily in the teens.

"Hi!" Olav bounces in the door as the jingle bells sound off his entrance. He rubs his upper arms furiously, but his smile doesn't fade from his face. Neither do the dimples that have made him a fan favorite with women of all ages.

I nod. "Decided to show up after all?"

He grins, blue eyes glinting with humor much like my mother's always do. "There's baked goods to be had, right?"

I roll my eyes. "Once we make them, yeah."

"Olav? Did you eat? Do you need a plate of Thorleif's lasagna?" My mother's voice sounds from the other side of the blanket. She can never help but spoil the man I'm pretty sure she considers her son. I don't mind sharing my mother, neither with Ragnhild nor with Olav.

The latter shoots me a smirk as he kicks his boots off. "Is the lasagna edible?"

I scoff. "Likely more than anything you have at home right now."

He laughs. "Yeah, that's for sure." He ducks under the wool blanket separating the porch from the living room and is immediately enveloped in my mother's one-armed hug. She sets the full plate on the table in front of him, and Olav winks at me. "It was nice knowing you."

I shake my head and drop down into the seat across from him. Olav isn't all that bad. Much as his family situation left him at a disadvantage—my aunt leaving him high and dry just a few years before his dad died—he seems to have recovered well.

He takes his first bite. "This isn't too bad, Thorleif. I guess it's not your cooking skills that are keeping the women away."

I roll my eyes. "I thought it was that you got to them first."

Olav grins, but stuffs more lasagna in his mouth rather than answer. It's an old joke that Olav is as much of a player as I am perpetually single. But maybe that will change soon? I don't have the blonde curls or massive dimples that have always paved the way for Olav. But then I'm also interested in the one woman in the world who has never given Olav the time of day.

Maybe, just maybe, I can still convince my fake bride to consider something more permanent in the next eight days.

CHAPTER 6

RAGNHIL

The Vaage house is all lit up for the holidays when Ingrid and I pull up to the house. String lights trim the doors and windows of the farmhouse, and traditional gingerbread hearts hang from red ribbons in the middle of each small-paned window.

I spent almost every school vacation, and most of December, with Thorleif's family, so I grew up with the same Norwegian traditions as he did—St. Lucia Day on December 13th is one of them.

"Are these the yellow rolls we've baked before?" Ingrid tucks her knit shawl tighter around her body. Apart from Thorleif, she's probably my best friend in the world, but she's not often at the Vaage house with me. And I may or may not have asked her mainly to be my buffer tonight. The tension between Thorleif and me has been unbearable lately.

It's not that I'm attracted to him, and I definitely don't want to kiss him. But sometimes my body seems to forget that the crush we have is on Jacob at work, not the stoic Viking look-alike I grew up with. The one who lately has had way too much heat burning in his eyes when he looks at me. I'll only be single for another eight days, and I need to keep my priorities straight.

I pull myself out of those memories and back into my conversation with Ingrid. "Yeah. If you baked yellow rolls with me, they were definitely *Lussekatter*. Shaped like cats and babies." I put the car in park and grin. "And the less traditional crocodile."

She nods, pushes a strand of her long, blonde hair away from her face, and narrows her blue eyes. "And it's you and me, Thorleif, and Olav?"

"That's the whole gang." I jump out of the car before the icy cold air infiltrates the inside of the cab, and Ingrid is quick to follow. The outside light clicks on as we cross the driveway.

As I pull the door open, I notice one of the gingersnap hearts in the window by the door has a bite taken out of it. I press my lips together to stifle my laugh as I kick off my boots.

Ingrid shuts the door behind us and stares at the teeth marks in the cookie heart. Then she turns wide eyes on me. "Who would…. Who would take a bite out of a window decoration? Are there little kids around here that I don't know of?"

I shake my head and push the blanket to the side. "Just that one over there." I tilt my head towards the large bearded man who doesn't look at all like a kid where he stands next to his equally tall and broad-shouldered, blonde cousin.

"Olav?" Ingrid crinkles her nose and laughs, but her laugh is just high-pitched enough that I can tell she's nervous. But surely not about Olav? I'm almost certain she's met him before.

"Nope. The other one—Thorleif."

"Oh." She looks away, but not before I see her pinking cheekbones. Which guy is causing the blush in her cheeks? Olav or Thorleif?

The guys turn, and Thorleif's face lights up when he sees us— when he sees me. "You're here!"

Does he always greet me like this? Or am I overanalyzing our every interaction because of the other night in the field? What if these signs have been here all along? How long have I ignored them?

A niggle of guilt tightens my stomach.

What if he really does have feelings for me and I've asked him to fake a wedding with me? I push the guilt down—it's just the normal tension between adult friends of the opposite sex, right?

"We're here! Hi Olav." I aim an exaggerated wave at both of them. But Olav doesn't even respond to my greeting—his attention is entirely focused on the girl next to me. The girl who meets his intense gaze head-on. I raise my eyebrows. That's...unexpected.

I glance at Thorleif. Am I the only one sensing the sparks between these two? Thorleif looks from Olav to Ingrid, rolls his eyes, and turns to walk into the kitchen.

Leaving the two of them to whatever stalemate they're caught in, I follow him.

An hour later, the kitchen is filled with the scent of rising yeast dough, freshly baked Lucia buns, and burned raisins. And Olav and Ingrid haven't stopped bickering, or more accurately flirting, since they entered the house. The attraction between them is laughably obvious. Olav has always been a bit of a flirt, but Ingrid is holding her own in this match which surprises me as much as it delights Olav.

"You call that a *Lussekatt*? I'm pretty sure my cat could have made a better one." Olav's blue eyes dance with mischief as he takes in the yellow lump of dough in Ingrid's hands.

Ingrid studies her handiwork, undeterred by the bait in his voice. "You have a cat?" The tone in her voice could almost pass for indifference. Almost. But I know her well enough to know that if *she* was a cat, her tail would be twitching.

Olav's eyes sparkle. "I don't. But if I did, I'm sure it could have done better."

Ingrid rolls her eyes and places the lumpy figure onto the parchment paper-covered, blackened cookie sheet next to him. Before she turns back, her eyes linger a moment too long on the broad shoulders stretching his Henley shirt. And I don't blame her for admiring the view.

Both Olav and Thorleif have the bone structure of their Norwegian ancestors. But where Thorleif's is well-hidden by his thick, dark beard, Olav's high cheekbones are on full display—and they're a work of art.

That said, I know which cousin I'd choose. My pulse skitters. I frown—not that I would choose either.

Thorleif bumps my shoulder with his elbow, and when I look up, his dark eyes are searching my face. "What's the frown for?"

I open my mouth to answer, but what could I possibly say? I feel my face heat as I wave my hand in the direction of the lovebirds. "Just… that."

Thorleif raises his eyebrows. "Just that, huh?"

Face flaming, I turn back to the current disagreement at the table.

Ingrid's eyes are narrowed. They're as blue as Olav's, but her hair is a shade blonder than his. "Have you made anything at all, or are you just criticizing people who actually pull their weight around here?"

Olav crosses his arms, jaw set in a mock scowl. "I only criticize poor workmanship." He flicks a lump of flour toward her.

Ingrid gasps and shakes the white powder off her hands. "Did you throw flour at me?"

The expression of angelic innocence on his face is sure to have gotten him out of a scrape or two when he was younger. "Who, me? I would never."

Ingrid sticks her tongue out at him—I think she's running out of comebacks. I glance at Thorleif to see if he's laughing, too—but he is watching me again.

My stomach does a somersault, which it's absolutely not supposed to do! I've never reacted to his attention this way before, so why would I now?

43

Olav's loud laugh pulls my attention back to him and Ingrid. "What's so funny?"

Ingrid shrugs and rolls her eyes. "Olav being immature as usual."

"Hey!" His shoulder bumps into hers in what I think is supposed to be a joking gesture, but he lingers in her space a little too long.

Oh, he's so done for.

Not that I blame him. Ingrid is kind and sweet, with long blonde hair and blue eyes that speak of her Nordic ancestry. She's like the real-life version of the princesses in the Norwegian folktales I read growing up. And the two of them obviously share a sense of humor.

I'd be worried if I wasn't so sure she knows enough about his reputation to keep her wits about her.

Ingrid pretends to focus on re-shaping her *Lussekatt* into a braided version of "the child" as pictured in Mor Vaage's red checkered cookbook laying open on the table.

Olav steps even closer, eyes narrowing in mock disgust. "*I'm* immature?"

Ingrid whips toward him, and for a few seconds, it seems she's forgotten where she is. Her gaze drops to his lips, and for the space of a breath I think they'll actually kiss right in front of Thorleif, me, and the *Lussekatt* rolls.

But then she pushes him away. "Aren't you always?"

Olav regains his composure faster than Ingrid. "Well, at least I'm not sticking my tongue out like I'm in elementary school."

She rolls her eyes and drops her last *Lussekatt* onto the tray. "I was homeschooled, so I didn't learn about that."

"You were not homeschooled!" He's back at her side, rolling his eyes, and it will be a true Christmas miracle if they make it through the night without kissing.

I steal a glance at Thorleif, and thankfully this time he's watching Olav and Ingrid's mating dance, too.

"At least they're pretty entertaining."

He grunts, but his eyes crinkle at the corners.

Across the table, Ingrid pushes Olav again. "Do you know this because you're *still* in elementary?"

Olav swipes his thumb down Ingrid's cheek, leaving a powdery, white streak. Then he jumps away before she has a chance to retaliate.

She gasps, and swipes a palm down her cheek, decimating only half of the flour.

Olav purses his lips, and his dancing eyes are only for her. "You should keep it. It suits you. Goes well with—" he waves a hand at the large, frilly apron Mor Vaage let her borrow "—whatever that is."

Ingrid grabs a handful of flour and takes a step towards Olav. "You know, now that you say it, I feel like your outfit is missing something, too."

He shrinks back, but not far enough. When he ducks away, Ingrid pounces lightning-fast to slip her hand down the back of his shirt. From the flour drizzling out the bottom of his shirt, it's pretty clear that hand wasn't empty.

Thorleif lets out a booming laugh, and I can't help but join in.

"Are you.... What the—" Olav whips on Ingrid, crowding her space. His fingers dig into her upper arms, but as much as she squirms, she's going nowhere. The inches between them narrow. Their faces tilt, narrowed eyes intent on the others'. The tension grows as they hold still.

I roll my eyes at their antics, but I know my smile slips into my voice. "Hey, guys, what's going on over there?"

"I'm winning a staring contest." Ingrid's attention stays locked on Olav's.

I raise my eyebrows. "Really? It looks like you're about to kiss."

Ingrid grimaces, but she never looks away from Olav's taunting, blue eyes. "Yeah, that's definitely not what's happening here."

Olav smirks. "You wish."

And I'm one hundred percent certain they'll end up lip-locked by the end of the night.

45

The oven timer beeps, interrupting the entertainment, and Thorleif moves to pull the second tray out of the oven.

Our crocodile sits proudly in the middle of the tray—in a puddle of burnt raisins. The crocodile isn't among the traditional Lussekatt shapes in Mor Vaage's red checkered cookbook—just a remnant from Thorleif and my shared childhood at the Vaage house.

I can't remember if it started because Thorleif was obsessed with crocodiles or because I wanted to put as many raisins as humanly possible on the dough—so more would fall off onto the tray. Either way, to this day, the crocodile with its row of shiny raisin teeth, and the even longer row of shiny raisin spikes across its back and tail, is a Lussekatt staple at the Vaage house.

I have no idea when, or why, the blackened, burnt raisins turned into my favorites. I lean closer to Thorleif and swipe a few off the tray before he's even set it down.

"Ragnhild! It's hot!" His growl doesn't deter me. In fact, I kind of want him to do it again.

I push away the thought and chew my burnt raisins. The sharp, sweet flavor fills me with feelings of nostalgia and home.

"Enjoying your charcoal treats?" The last tray is in the oven, so Thorleif must have convinced the bickering children to give it up. Now he's staring at me.

And, as much as I tell my pulse there's no need to speed up—it's just Thorleif—I don't really want him to look away.

And that? That's a problem.

CHAPTER 7

THORLEIF

December 14th

Bright morning sunlight dances across the snowy front lawn, through the wavy window panes, and onto the page of the book in my hand. A fire is crackling in the *Jøtul* stove, and the scent of fresh coffee tinges the warm air around me.

I take another sip from the steaming cup in my hand and place it back down on the table as I let out a contented sigh. For a Saturday in the middle of December, it's as perfect as it can be.

Well, almost as perfect as it could be.

Ragnhild, having stayed overnight since last night's *Lussekatt* baking, is here somewhere, too. And while I'm comfortable as I am, sprawled on the couch in the living room, having her here next to me is the only improvement I can imagine. And I have imagined it a time or two already this morning.

She stumbled downstairs earlier with her red hair falling haphazardly out of her hair clip, rubbing her tired eyes—looking good enough to eat. As she always does.

Unfortunately, Bestemor picked up her black and white knitting project and left for the backroom as soon as Ragnhild entered.

My chest still aches from the dejection on Ragnhild's face as she watched Bestemor's back. I desperately wish I had the power to fix the rift between them, but I don't think I do.

Ragnhild moved past me shortly after, mumbling something about needing to clean up. But the shower stopped a while ago, so I should be seeing her soon.

Balancing my book in one hand, I reach again for the steaming cup of coffee on the table. I just barely have time to swallow my sip before light footsteps sound across the hardwood floor. And then Ragnhild is there—long hair flowing over the shoulders of her traditional Norwegian *lusekofte* sweater, and for a moment I forget how to breathe.

"Good morning, Thorleif." Her voice is a bit scratchy as if she hasn't used it much yet today. And why would she have? My mother is at work, and Bestemor and I are the only people at home.

Ragnhild's spun copper hair, dark jeans, and red *lusekofte* already make me hold tighter to the coffee mug in my hand as I swallow down my desire. But then she smiles at me—blue eyes shining and face glowing, and I'm lost to the world.

All I can do is take in everything about her. The way her knit sweater clings to her movements. The way she cradles the coffee mug in her hands. The scent of her shower gel—wait! I actually think that's my shower gel. Why did she use my shower gel when there are several choices in there marketed towards women? Did my mother and Bestemor's products run out? Does she just like the way it smells? I want to decipher the meaning behind that if there is one.

But then the pale winter sun beams through the window panes and light on her face as she leans forward to put her coffee on the table. And all thoughts of shower gel leave my mind.

Ragnhild kneels next to the low table. Her pink tongue slips out to wet her lips, and my stomach tightens. Her fingers unsuccessfully brush away copper strands from her face as she puts the mug to her lips, tilting it just slightly. Her throat bobs, and her pale lashes lower as she revels in that first sip with a dreamy expression on her face.

I've watched her take her first sip of coffee in the morning a million times before, and still, I can't get enough. I can never get enough.

Her eyebrows rise, and her eyes are knowing as she catches me staring.

My neck feels hot, and I force a *good morning* past the tightness in my throat. The words come out all croaky and weird, but Ragnhild just laughs. A glittery laugh that warms places inside me I didn't know existed.

"Morning to you, too." She puts her cup back down on the table and pushes up from the floor. Then she plops down on the couch beside me, making my coffee splash dangerously up the sides of my cup. I drop the cup to the table before I soak either of us in hot coffee. Not that it would up my temperature much. I'm feeling plenty hot with embarrassment.

Ragnhild reaches for her cup again, and I pick my book back up. I open it to the bookmarked spot and let my eyes follow the words down the page. I turn the page and scan down the next one. But it's all pretense. I think the main character is in some sort of epic battle, but I'm only half-concentrated on the story I'm reading. How can I be anything else when Ragnhild's happy voice floats in the air around me?

My heart feels buoyant and light in my chest as I listen to her. And I know beyond a shadow of a doubt that I want every Saturday morning to be like this. Every morning the rest of the week, too. Every morning for the foreseeable future with a laughing Ragnhild next to me sounds like paradise. She leans over to grab a book from the coffee table, and her hair brushes my cheek. I breathe in just then and am rewarded with a mouthful of hair.

"Ragnhild, what the—" I pull copper strands out of my mouth.

She laughs again, and her laughter is a pure shot of happiness through my veins. Who'd need caffeine if they had this girl?

I reach for her, but she squeals and scrambles away. She knows that if I catch her, I'll tickle her until laughter steals her breath. It's happened more than once, and I've yet to lose.

I grunt. "You're lucky I'm too tired to chase you right now."

She rolls her eyes and puffs out a breath that sends more of her beautiful hair flying.

But her guard is down, and it's all the opening I need.

Quick as lightning, I wrap my arms around her, and my hands travel up her sweater to her waist, where I know she's the most ticklish. I dig my fingers into her waist, and she howls my name.

She wriggles loose, but she's not free for long. My arm is around her, pulling her back to me as my leg hooks over hers as an extra safety measure.

She gasps. "Thorleif, please"—another gasp—"I can't breathe."

My arms slacken immediately, and she turns, quick hands going for my armpits.

I growl. "So much for showing you mercy, huh?"

I try to grasp her hands, but she's using her full strength, and my girl isn't weak. Plus, she has the added advantage that I'm worried about hurting her. She, on the other hand, has no such qualms. Signified by the painful elbow to my gut. "Alright, mercy."

My words are a grunt, but her fingers are merciless.

Her tricks, however, are twenty years old at this point, and I know each and every one of them. It takes me no more than a second to get the upper hand again. Or more accurately, to have both of my hands wrapped around her wrists, both knees on either side of her hips.

I narrow my eyes at my still-wriggling best friend. "Truce?"

Her blue eyes, sweet and innocent when they want to be, narrow right back. I raise my eyebrows. She pushes out another breath, blowing a part in the hair mostly covering her face now. "Fine! Truce."

I transfer her wrists to one of my hands, and push away the hair from her face, so I can see her eyes. I narrow my eyes as I stare deeply into hers, my face a mere inch away as I try to decipher her level of honesty.

Her warm breath mingles with mine.

And suddenly, our tickle fight is no longer at the forefront of my mind. Not with me all but straddling her, and her beautiful face in kissing distance. I swallow hard, and my gaze makes a quick detour to her lips before it returns to her wide eyes.

I think she's come to the same conclusion as I—that if anyone saw us now, they would *not* think we were having a tickle fight. We probably look like we're halfway through a makeout session—chests heaving and hair wild.

My pulse quickens at the thought.

But pink spreads across Ragnhild's cheekbones, and her eyes drop quickly from mine.

The minute I let her go she scrambles off out from under me and off the couch. She doesn't even glance my way until she's sitting, legs tucked up under her, in the chair next to the couch. A very safe distance away.

I frown. "Are you alright? Did I hurt you?"

She shakes her head vigorously. "No! I'm fine, everything is fine." Right it is. Her voice is a full octave higher than usual, and the laugh she pushes out is not the same carefree sound as before.

I shrug and pretend to settle back in with my book, knowing I can't push her now. But oh, how desperately I want to know what's going on in her head. Is she as affected by our compromising position as I am? Or is she unsettled because she genuinely only feels friendship for me?

Whatever the reason, she's embarrassed. If I know her right, she'll soon make up an excuse to go to the backroom to grab a book from her secret romance novel stash. The one that isn't really a secret at all, since we all know about it. Well, my mother and Bestemor, and I know about it. Ragnhild, however, still thinks it's a secret.

A minute later, she pops up from her seat. "I'm…. I'm going to check on the space heater. I don't remember if I left it on."

She hasn't even been in the backroom today and definitely hasn't been fiddling with the space heater. But I grunt an answer into my coffee. Then, I stay very quiet as she moves through the backroom door. Quiet enough that I hear her groan as she opens the lid of the wood box.

I stuck *Falling in Love With My Best Friend* not so conspicuously at the top of the stack last night before I went to bed—I suspect that is the reason for the groan.

All that remains now, is figuring out if that was a good groan or a bad one. And what that distinction means for the future I want with her.

CHAPTER 8

RAGNHILD

December 15th, the third Sunday of Advent

It's been a full twenty-four hours since the tickle fight that turned from supremely innocuous to...not that. My face still feels hot, as if the embarrassment hasn't stopped coursing through my veins since then. But that embarrassment is accompanied by another much more disconcerting emotion—desire.

I'm in my car driving over to the Vaage house, nerves bouncing around in my stomach at the thought of seeing Thorleif again so soon.

It is so wrong. So, so wrong. But I'd be lying if I didn't admit that a tiny part of me—we're talking teeny tiny, and definitely indiscernible to the human eye—wanted to lean forward yesterday, and....

My eyes drop shut for just a moment while dismay, or disappointment, fills the sigh I let out.

I wanted to kiss Thorleif.

I wanted to kiss a man who's basically my brother. Sure, I know we're not actually related, but we grew up together. We've been best friends forever. I've just asked him to stage a wedding with me. Because I'm interested in another man. A man who's also interested in me.

I fan myself remembering the flirtatious glint in Jacob's eyes as he told me to have a good weekend on Thursday. There were definitely sparks flying, and I have no doubt that we're meant for each other. We have the same quirky sense of humor, we both like waffles. Twice, I've caught him gazing at me when he thought I wasn't looking. And honestly, when a girl has a man look at her like that she's going to want to lock him down. It's been months of him never making a move, so what better way to make that happen than a fake wedding?

Romance novels and romantic movies are positively overflowing with wedding ceremonies where former lovers jump up from their seats when the minister says, *"Speak now or forever hold your peace."* Sure, it's a cliche. But cliches are that for a reason.

The hardest part should have been finding a fake groom, and I've got that part down, so what else could really go wrong?

Apart from suddenly developing a questionable desire to kiss your best friend?

Nothing.

I groan and cover my face with my hand. The car veers to the right of the snowy road, and I immediately drop my hand and straighten the steering wheel. Driving is more important than the physical expression of my emotional upheaval. After all, my journey to the altar might be cut short quickly if I end up in a ditch today.

I manage to stay out of the ditch on the entire twenty-minute drive to Thorleif's house. He comes outside as soon as I pull into his driveway which is more mud than snow.

As soon as I exit the car the tension between us turns thicker than Norwegian *rømmegrøt*. I turn around, crack open my car door, and dig in the pile of coats and blankets in the front seat of my car. Triumphantly, I pull out the piece of poorly photocopied paper that is the solution to all my guy troubles. The paper proof that I need to keep my wits about me only for another six days. Once Jacob and I are going out, I'm certain the relationship between me and Thorleif will go back to normal.

"I got the license!" I brandish the fake marriage license as if it's my one and only claim to fame. Thorleif takes it, an unreadable expression on his face as his dark eyes scan the paper from top to bottom.

I wait for him to say something, but he only dips his head and hands the paper back to me. Then he launches into a story about a guy he works with.

I wiggle my toes inside my thick winter boots. I can't read his thoughts, and Bjørn's antics last weekend don't explain what I want to know.

The sun is out, but the warmth of it against my face only makes me feel more antsy, not less. Isn't Thorleif at all worried about the validity of the license? Or does he not care either way?

I interrupt him, waving the marriage license a bit too enthusiastically in his face. "It's not on file with the town clerk, so it's not possible for it to be valid."

Yes, I've read enough of those books, and I'm not going to put myself, or Thorleif, in that position. I search for the relief on his face, but all I see is his brows tugged down into a frown. His voice is reproachful. "Ragnhild. Were you even listening to me?"

I grimace, kicking at a leaf frozen halfway into a muddy lump of ice before I look back up at him. "I was! I just thought it was important that you knew we wouldn't accidentally end up married."

He scoffs, brows dipping even lower over his eyes. "Yes, being saddled with me for the rest of your life would be quite the travesty." His voice is dry, and way too serious for his words.

My mouth falls open in shock. I have never heard Thorleif sound this...self-deprecating? What has gotten into him?

"I mean, it wouldn't be ideal, but..." His thundering glare makes me end that sentence before it has time to materialize between us. "What is wrong? I thought you'd be relieved?"

He runs a frustrated hand through his hair, making it stand adorably on end. I want to reach out to fold it back down, but I pin my hands to my side. I'm determined to keep them to myself, no matter how much they want to wander.

Which they don't.

Thorleif's eyes narrow. "Do you really think so little of yourself?"

I roll my eyes. "I don't think little of myself." How can he say that? I'm staging a wedding to force the man I want to ask me out. That is one hundred percent main character energy.

But Thorleif crosses his arms, downright scowling now. "For someone who thinks so highly of herself, you're going to an awful lot of trouble turning the head of a guy who hasn't bothered to ask you out over the several months you've worked together."

He's not right. He's not! Jacob is just shy. He *does* like me.

I fold my arms over my chest. "He just needs a push in the right direction, that's all." I don't want to fight with Thorleif. Especially not when his words hit so close to home. He's right that Jacob has had plenty of chances to ask me out and hasn't yet. But surely seeing me get married will change that?

It will.

I stare at the marriage license trembling in my hand. Even without being filed, it was enough for the secretary at the Seamen's Church to add our names to the last-minute opening on the wedding calendar—three days before Christmas Eve.

I'd told the minister officiating that we'd already gone through our premarital counseling with the minister at our own church, and he didn't ask for confirmation.

So in addition to upsetting my best friend, I've also lied to my superior at work. I wince. Who am I even becoming?

Thorleif paces the muddy driveway in front of me. Getting him on board had been the most difficult, least predictable part. And somehow it hadn't been all that hard. A hand on his arm and an imploring look, and he'd melted. Sure, he hadn't agreed immediately, but I'd known he would eventually.

Until now. Now, I'm suddenly not so sure anymore.

I clear my throat. "Are you…. Are you saying you don't want to go through with this?"

He pauses his movements, hesitating. His brown eyes find mine, and I hold them until the honesty I see there becomes too much. I drop my eyes to where my boots are planted firmly in the muddy slush.

"No."

My heart sinks. His words are so final, so hard, that I can't help the tears welling in my eyes. "I'm sorry, I shouldn't have—"

He waves a large hand in front of my face, breaking my eye contact with the ground. I turn my attention back to his face instead. His eyes are dark and filled with emotions I can't decipher.

"No, Ragnhild. I'm saying that I'm not pulling out. If you want me to show up there on Saturday and pretend we're a happily engaged couple, I will."

He will? I sniff, feeling like a child for crying so easily. "Maybe not *too* happily."

The corner of his mouth tugs beneath his beard, and his eyes crinkle at the corners—just the way I love. "I promise not to look too happy."

"Thank you." A laugh slips over my lips, and I feel like the most emotionally unstable girl in the county, but I can't help it. Do they give out prizes for that? Miss Madison County's Most Emotionally Unstable Girl? I'd win with a landslide.

Thorleif clears his throat and holds up a hand, pulling me out of my pageant dreams. "Now, I'm not saying this isn't a terrible idea, or that I condone it in any way. But it's apparently important to you, so I'll help you pull it off."

He's a better friend than I am—by miles and bounds. But he always has been.

I chew on my lip as I consider his words. Thorleif's attention fastens on the movement, and I immediately let my lip go— pretending not to notice the somersault in my midsection at the way his eyes darken. "You don't think you're going to regret going along with this?"

He shrugs, but there's light and humor in his eyes now. "Probably."

I sigh as relief courses through me. My shoulders sink. "Thank you for doing it anyways."

He dips his head. And then, knowing me much too well, he opens his arms, and I dive into them. Not only is Thorleif a much better friend than me—he's much better than I deserve.

His strong arms wrap around me, and I press my cheek to his warm flannel-covered chest. His heartbeat quickens as I do so, and I try not to notice—try not to make any guesses as to why.

I press down my suspicion that he's only agreeing to this faux wedding because his feelings towards me are more than friendly. And I try not to feel like a massive jerk for letting him go through with it after all.

I don't like him that way—could never like him that way. I keep repeating the thought, needing my body to understand that this topsy-turvy feeling in my stomach isn't romantic feelings.

But held tightly in his arms like this, with the scent of woodsmoke, cardamom, and Thorleif surrounding me—it's not quite working.

Actually, it's not working at all.

CHAPTER 9

THORLEIF

The sweet scent of oranges melds with the spicy tang of the clove buds we've spent the last hour poking into them. The literal fruits of our labors sit in the middle of the large farmhouse table, and Ragnhild, finally, seems a bit more relaxed. At least more than when she showed up here this morning, as tense as a loaded spring while she held her fake marriage license out in front of herself like it was a wreath of garlic meant to ward off evil.

Except in her case, I'm going to assume it was meant to ward off my attraction to her. The attraction I'm increasingly certain she's aware of. Or maybe—my heart does a jump—it's meant to ward off her attraction to me. Or is that nothing more than a pipedream?

I watch her from the seat next to her on the old wooden bench. A small smile lingers on her lips as her nimble fingers tie another purple satin ribbon around the now spiky fruit. The scent of Ragnhild and the clove-studded oranges feels like the essence of home. I'm aware I'm literally inside my house, but I'm confident I could smell this particular aroma in a mall packed with frantic Christmas shoppers and I'd feel every bit at home.

The lull in conversation is easy, but I want to know what she's thinking. If that fake marriage license is making her rethink her fake wedding plans.

And what better way than to jolt her out of her reverie?

"Are we going to have to kiss?" I ask the question innocently, pretending I don't care either way. As if I wouldn't jump on the chance to kiss the girl next to me. But Ragnhild's reaction is worth any hesitation I might have felt asking.

She gasps, fumbles with the satin ribbon, drops the orange, and turns to me with eyes as wide as saucers. The forgotten orange rolls down the table and thuds against the floor as her gaze travels frantically around the room. Next, she slams her hand over my mouth, practically landing in my lap with the effort to shut me up.

"Are you out of your mind?" Her breath is as hot as the angry words she whisper-shouts straight into my ear.

Her fingers pressed to my mouth are sticky and smell like orange peel. But I'm not going to complain about the way she's all but climbed on top of me to stop me from spilling our secrets. Not when her silky ponytail slides over the skin of my neck, making goose bumps break out across my skin.

All of her is warm and soft and perfect, and I love how she feels against me.

I'm fairly certain both my mother and Bestemor are out of earshot in the backroom, which is the only reason I asked the question. That, and maybe to get a rise out of Ragnhild—and I definitely got that.

She drops her hand, but my mouth still feels sticky from her orange-scented fingers. "You can't say those things here! What if anyone heard you?"

I drop my voice. "You know as well as I do that it's a reasonable question. If I'm going to be a convincing *slightly unhappy* fake fiance I need to know where your boundaries are."

Hopefully, they don't rule out kissing, but if they do, she'll need to clarify it. I frown, is it even realistic that we'd be engaged and not kiss at all while we're in the building we're about to get married in?

"Alright, but there won't be any kissing." Her voice is barely a whisper.

"None at all?" I know she just shot me down, but my pulse speeds up at the thought of kissing her. It wouldn't even need to be a real kiss—I'd go for just touching her lips to mine. Just holding her the way I'm aching to would be a relief.

"No!" She hisses the words, and her vehement disagreement is a little insulting. Surely she doesn't think I'm a terrible kisser?

But if kissing is not on the menu, what is? She's not expecting me to keep my hands completely to myself, is she? If we're going to make it look like we're about to get married, we'd have to be touching a little.

I still at a sudden creak from behind me. It's not the creaking of the backroom door, is it? I don't really want Ragnhild off my lap, but I also don't want to be the one explaining to Bestemor why she is on top of me, so....

I move my hands to her waist, and she jumps off of me as if my hands are icicles touching her bare skin. Well, that was easy. I'm guessing *hands on waist* isn't included on the approved physical contact list.

After a quick peek over my shoulder at the still-shut backroom door, I lower my voice a bit. "If we're not kissing, then what are we doing? People who are about to get married generally have some sort of romantic relationship—a physical relationship."

But now Ragnhild looks a bit green about the gills, and I immediately regret starting the conversation. This is new territory for me, but I don't know if it's as new for Ragnhild. Does she have scars I don't know about? "You don't honestly think I'd push you into something you're not comfortable with, do you?"

I feel sick to my stomach already, but she quickly shakes her head. "It's not that. I just.... I really need us to not let any of this slip to Mor Vaage or Bestemor."

I frown, surveying the clove-studded oranges on the table in front of us while I gather my thoughts. I reach out to tug on the ribbons of the two already wrapped with purple silk ribbons, ready to hang from the curtain rods in the windows.

I thought this was about us touching, not my mother and grandmother. "Why?"

Her eyes widen, and her face gets very loud. "What do you mean why? Because they'd marry us off for real before you'll have had time to as much as *look* for a ring. You'd turn around one morning, and we'd be on our honeymoon in Fiji."

She says this last part as if it's a catastrophe the equivalent of the Irish famine. Does she really have no idea about the grin I'm suppressing at the mere idea of imagining a honeymoon in Fiji—with her? Quite frankly any honeymoon with her anywhere. I'd take a tent in the field up on the hill.

But I do suppress it and shrug. "Fiji doesn't sound half bad. I'm assuming they'd pay. I could do with a vacation, to be honest."

She groans, pressing two fingers into the spot between her eyebrows. "Thorleif, be serious. We can't let them think we're together for real when they've been dropping hints since you were a senior in high school."

Wait, what? Really? "That long?" I must be more oblivious than I thought.

Ragnhild rolls her eyes. "Yeah, definitely that long. And if we tell them it was all a joke...." She swallows thickly. "I might not be welcome here at all anymore."

Her smile doesn't quite reach her eyes, and her little laugh sounds strangled at best.

I know she's trying to make it sound like a joke, but I also know that this particular joke sits quite close to the truth.

Ragnhild's mother never took her role very seriously—and truthfully, that woman never deserved the responsibility. I've always known that part of the reason Ragnhild and I have stayed so close is Ragnhild's lack of her own family. She's been my friend, yes, but she's also been the daughter my mother never had—and Bestemor's granddaughter.

I wait until her eyes reluctantly find mine, and erase all traces of humor from my voice. "You'll always be welcome here, Ragnhild. This house is as much yours as it is mine. As is my family."

She stills. Her eyes turn glassy before they drop to her lap. Her fingers pull on a loose string on her yellow sweater. "You think so?"

I shake my head, and my fingers cover hers. "I know so."

The scent of oranges and cloves still lingers in the air as her chest rises and falls with each heaving breath. I rub my thumb back and forth over the top of her hand while she struggles through the pain of old wounds she never deserved. Finally, her hand turns over in her lap, and her fingers curl around mine. When she does meet my eyes, tears spill over her pale lashes to trace down her freckled cheeks.

I wish I could kiss them away, but I slide them away with the thumb of my other hand instead. "I'm not trying to jeopardize your place in this family, Ragnhild. Not in the slightest."

She sniffs and nods. "I know that. I just. I can't…." Her voice is tremulous and teary and it pulls on my heartstrings. I would do anything for her. Anything. Including stepping back from my feelings for as long as she needs me to.

"I am just trying to clarify your boundaries. If we're not kissing, and I can't touch you, how are we supposed to sell the relationship?"

She rubs her palm across her eyes and sniffs again. "I'm not entirely sure. But I mean, we don't have to sell it for very long. It will mostly just be us as we get ready and stuff."

I nod. "But I can hold your hand and open your doors, stuff like that?"

She smiles a teary smile that makes my chest fill with the need to go out and conquer the world. For her. "You already do those things."

Yes, because I already love you. And in my heart, you're already the girl I want to marry.

And maybe—my heart jolts at the thought—just maybe, she'll realize that one day soon.

"Just...." Ragnhild hesitates. "I guess any little touches are fine, like my back and shoulders and stuff. Just don't grope me or try to kiss me."

I grimace. Does she really think I'd try that? While knowing full well that she doesn't want me to? I'm speechless for a moment.

Ragnhild laughs, swiping at the errant wetness still on her cheeks. "You look so offended right now."

I clear my throat. "Why? Why would I not be offended that you think I'd act like that—groping you in a church on your wedding day, against your will? Do you know me at all?"

She laughs again. "I do know you. And I don't think you would, but I just wanted to make it very, very clear."

She leans over, close to my face, invading my space in the best way. Her breath smells sweet, and her face smells like oranges. "Thank you for being the kind of man I can trust."

And then her warm lips press against my cheek. It's quick. No more than a peck.

It's over so fast it might not have happened at all.

But it did.

And I think I might have died and gone to heaven. Maybe my dream girl isn't as far out of reach as I think?

CHAPTER 10

RAGNHILD

One of my earliest memories is sitting awake in the dark hallway outside my mom's bedroom—terrified to get yelled at if I woke her up. And more terrified still to go back to the little room where I'd awakened from a nightmare.

I've spent most of my life since hating the thought of what lurks in the darkness beyond the circle of light from the window. It's not even 5 pm, and the New York countryside is already shrouded in darkness beyond the flimsy pane of glass.

I'm too old to imagine monsters, but it doesn't keep me from picturing staring, beady eyes watching me. Or the accompanying clawed hands reaching out.

I tuck closer to the man beside me. The man whose warm forearm rests against mine, settling my racing pulse. With him next to me, the velvety dark outside doesn't feel quite as much like a threat.

I watch Thorleif out of the corner of my eye. His plaid button-down shirt spans his wide shoulders as he sits hunched at the table. I'm sure Mor Vaage has given up on making him straighten his back while he eats by now.

With my eyes, I trail the raised veins that map the surface of his hands and wrists from long days of physical labor. His thick, strong fingers rest on the table next to mine—so close it would take a very slight movement from me to tuck my hand in his. Just like I did earlier.

I tighten my fist, suddenly worried I'll reach out and do just that.

I spent the majority of my day with Thorleif at this very farmhouse table poking clove buds into fresh oranges. And even though we likely could have been much more effective in the use of our time, the quite literal fruits of our labor now hang from purple satin ribbons next to the gingerbread hearts in all of the windows in the room.

But then, of course, he had to go and ask me if we would be kissing. Just the thought sends a tingle through my stomach, just like it did then. Not because I want to kiss Thorleif, because of course I don't—and even yesterday morning it was only a temporary blip of desire. But why is all the evidence pointing to him wanting to kiss me?

Moving my attention back up to his face, I catch the familiar hint of a smile hidden behind his full beard. I know he can't know what I'm thinking about, and that that's not why he's smiling like that—but I blush all the same.

Another thought strikes as suddenly.

Because someday some other girl will fall in love with that hidden smile; the secrets in his eyes. She'll lace her fingers with Thorleif's—not as friends might sometimes do—but like lovers do. The thought sends a jolt through me, and some emotion I'm afraid to name stirs deep in my gut.

Why is the idea of Thorleif dating anyone seriously so disconcerting? It's not like I've expected Thorleif to stay single for the rest of his life. He is handsome, kind, and trustworthy—any girl who had the chance would be crazy for not snatching him up. And one day soon, someone will. It's quite a miracle that no one has already.

Thorleif will bring a girl home someday, I'm certain of this. But when? And what will she be like?

I've had no practice seeing him with girls. It's been years since I've seen him show interest in anyone, even longer since he's dated.

I think back to our moment at the table earlier. Is that why all this chemistry is popping up between us lately? Has it been so long since either of us have been in a relationship that our bodies are just malfunctioning?

I remember the tender way he wiped away the tears from my cheeks earlier.

"You'll always be welcome here, Ragnhild. This house is as much yours as it is mine. As is my family."

But will that really be true? Even when he brings another girl home? Will Mor Vaage still treat me like the daughter she never had, or will his girlfriend take my place?

And what will that girlfriend think of me? What if she tries to sabotage my friendship with Thorleif out of jealousy? Will he let her?

A burning ache stirs in my chest.

Mor Vaage's strong voice pulls my attention back to the here and now as a match bursts into flame. She lights the candle, pulls the match away, and shakes her hand to extinguish it.

One of the purple candles in the candle wreath centerpiece is already lit, and two more have blackened wicks. The fourth will be lit on the last Sunday before Christmas.

In one week.

Bestemor and Mor Vaage both sing the traditional candle-lighting hymn—mother and daughter's voices harmonizing the slow, beautiful tune.

Next to me, Thorleif suddenly winces, then half-heartedly joins their voices with his dark timbre. When his voice fades, the bench shakes, and he grunts and winces again.

Mor Vaage's eyes are full of mischief across the table. Not unlike her son's eyes, mid-tickle fights in years past. Definitely nothing like his eyes during the one we had yesterday.

Goosebumps trail my spine as I remember the heat burning in

his eyes as his gaze fell to my mouth. I panicked, scrambling out from under him and excusing myself to the backroom and my secret book stash. But the book at the top of my reading pile was not one I'd put there. And reading a best friends to lovers story was precisely *not* what I needed at that moment in time.

Or ever.

Not when I am not only *not falling in love* with my best friend, but rather using his goodwill for me to snatch up another man. I dug down to find an office romance instead—one with much safer fictional crushes.

The melody around me continues as another flash of light blazes in the December night, and one more blackened wick blossoms into a bright flame. Another verse of the hymn, and one more stifled wince from the man next to me before his deep baritone joins in.

I don't think Norwegian sons are allowed to be anything but decent singers. How can they, when so many of the traditional rituals include singing?

I try to swallow my laugh at the torment in Thorleif's expression. He sends me a glare, eyebrows lowered over dark eyes. My breath catches, but not because I think he's actually mad. Angry Thorleif is kind of hot—

Wait what?

No, he's not. I push the ridiculous idea away with a brilliant smile directed at my best friend; my only ever that.

"Just sing! It can't be that hard!" I mouth the words to him and delight in the way his eyes darken. It's not as if singing three short verses will kill him. Then again, he's an adult and can pick his mother's scolding kicks if that's what he prefers.

Thorleif lets out a breath of relief when all three candles are lit, and all three verses sung. I can't help but let out a loud cackle of laughter. Thorleif sends another scowl in my direction. "You should be singing too."

I gape, eyes wide and innocent. "I should not! I don't even speak Norwegian, and you know it!"

The look he sends me tells me he's not fooled by my innocent mask. Thorleif is lucky enough to be bilingual, Bestemor having moved to the U.S. when Mor Vaage was a teenager. With all the hours I've spent at their house, I've picked up quite a bit of Norwegian, too. Especially any words around Christmas and Advent. I've spent almost the full month of December here since the year I started kindergarten, and as many times as I've listened to these lyrics in particular, I could have followed them as easily as he does. And he knows it.

I bat my eyelashes at him, and his eyes narrow.

"Thorleif, your plate." Mor Vaage holds out her hand, brows raised. It's the look she's given us thousands of times before. I know it's a scolding one, but it warms my insides every time. My mother had scolding looks of her own, but never like this—none so steeped in love.

Thorleif's family home, his family, has been my safe haven for as long as I can remember. In my younger years, my mother's nomadic lifestyle made this house the only solid point in my life—a steady harbor.

I have my own apartment just twenty minutes away, but I'll never turn down a meal at this table if I can help it. And I don't.

Now that my mom is gone, they are my only family. Though maybe they've always been.

I pick at my food as the dark thoughts sludge around in my brain. I usually enjoy Thorleif being home at supper time, but not today. Today, I'm just too aware of his large body next to me on the wooden bench. His presence swirls my thoughts, making my stomach tighten in a way I absolutely need it not to.

In less than a week I'll put out my clothes for a fake wedding the next morning. Sitting next to my pretend groom now feels much like I've swallowed a swarm of butterflies. Is it normal to be nervous about a made-up wedding? If the ceremony is fake, shouldn't the nerves be as well?

And what about the latent desire from yesterday's tickle fight? Is that what I should be feeling? Am I fooling myself thinking our chemistry will go away once my fake wedding makes Jacob ask me out? Will Thorleif just...stop this—whatever it is he's doing?

Earlier when he asked if we needed to kiss, was the tightening in my stomach just part of this chemistry between two friends?

I try to imagine what this would be like if our engagement were real. If the man who wiped away my tears as if I was precious to him was the man I wanted to ask me out. If I hadn't scrambled off his lap, but let his hands tighten around my waist instead. If I'd kissed his lips rather than his cheekbone.

I swallow, because that image is not...half as bad as I thought it would be.

Jacob invades my thoughts, and I feel a stab of guilt. I shouldn't be imagining kissing my best friend when I want to date my coworker. Definitely should not be doing that.

Jacob and I are a match made in heaven, and he will not ruin my life if things don't work out between us. Thorleif on the other hand? If things went south between us, if I broke his heart, would he still let me spend all my evenings here? Would I even want to?

The man quietly devouring his meal by my side draws my attention again. What would he say if he knew what I was thinking? Would he calm my fears with a glance, with the steady presence he's had since he was a child?

Would he want to try?

My stomach bubbles with things I can't even describe. That I need to stop feeling.

When Jacob and I start dating, my relationship with Thorleif will go back to normal, won't it? Guilt niggles my stomach, souring the meatballs and potatoes I forked down less than a minute ago.

Thorleif is my best friend. Doesn't asking him to do this break all the best friend codes ever? What if my plan ruins our friendship? Will he regret going along with it and resent both me and Jacob?

I push my plate away, my appetite all but gone. What if I've made a huge mistake? What if bringing Jacob into the mix ruins every-thing? Will I be able to recover the damage?

I want to drop my forehead to the table and cry. Why didn't I think about what dating Jacob would do to my relationship with Thorleif before now?

CHAPTER 11

RAGNHILD

December 17th

On the 17th of December, Ingrid comes over to the Vaage house to bake gingersnaps with Thorleif and me. Would she be mad if she knew this is the second time I've asked her to come mainly so I'll have a buffer between me and Thorleif? Maybe.

But it's not like I have a choice. Whatever this tension between us is, it's getting out of hand. And it's not what I need with just four more days before our very fake wedding—four days that somehow both feel like an eternity away *and* a ticking time bomb.

We walk inside from the cold and pull off coats and winter boots. A red, heavy wool blanket separates the freezing porch from the living room where the *Jøtul* stove is doing its best to impart toasty Christmas cheer. When I pull the blanket to the side for Ingrid and me to walk through, the farmhouse table is already decked out with a red waxed tablecloth.

Thorleif grabs the giant pickle jar from the sideboard and pours a pile of flour into the middle of the table. He looks up as I walk in, his smile big and welcoming.

My cheeks heat, and my heart does a staccato little dance that has no place in this relationship. *Friends, little heart, Thorleif and I are friends.*

But my heart isn't listening.

"Hi." I smile back at him, then turn to Ingrid before he has a chance to start up a conversation. "Do you need to borrow an apron?"

She shrugs off her shoulder bag and rolls her eyes. "Yeah, I don't usually bring an apron in my bag." I frown at her prickly response. Ingrid isn't usually like this, although she's been quiet this week, barely answering my texts since Saturday morning.

Guilt stabs my middle. If I'd spent less time freaking out about my upcoming, and very fake, nuptials, I'd have had time to check in with her more. Maybe I can get what's bothering her out of her during the drive home tonight?

I walk past Thorleif to reach for two aprons from the rack on the back of the bathroom door at the end of the kitchen, and hand Ingrid one of them. I keep the blue-flowered, pale yellow one for myself. It's an old pinafore-style apron, like the ones worn by sturdy housewives in photos from the 1940s. I tug it over my head and reach for the ties.

"That's my great-grandmother's apron." Thorleif is suddenly right behind me, his warm, large hands snatching the apron strings right out of mine.

I squeak as my face flushes. "What are you doing?"

"Helping you tie your apron? Is there anything wrong with that?" There's confusion in his voice as he steps back, but he doesn't let go of the strings.

I turn to Ingrid who gives me a pained look, then shrugs her shoulders. Great, I'm the only one making a big deal out of this. "Go ahead, I guess."

I feel Thorleif's breath on my neck as he tightens the strings of the apron, subtly tugging me towards him. I bite my lip as his strong knuckles brush against my sweatshirt and he loops the strings into a bow. My stomach swirls, and I want to close my eyes and revel in the sensations. In him.

I feel his touch through the fabric of my clothes, and it burns as if his calluses are sliding across my bare back. I don't try to picture that in my mind, but the scene enters unbidden. I press my eyes closed to remove it.

This is Thorleif. He is my friend. Nothing more.

So why, when he must have done this a million times before, does it feel so intimate now? It makes no sense.

I need to find a way to control my rapid breathing. Somehow there has to be a way to slow the skittering pulse at my neck. He's tying my apron strings, for goodness sake!

Except, it's not just *that* he's doing, of course. He's standing too close, lingering too long, tying the ribbons too carefully for it not to be more. And it shouldn't affect me like this.

I feel faint when Thorleif finally pulls the bow tight and steps back. "All done."

I want to fan myself, but that would be stupid, so I squeeze out a *thanks*, instead. One that sounds exactly as flummoxed as I feel. Ingrid, who has managed to tie her own apron strings by tugging them around her waist and placing the bow in front, watches us curiously. "You guys ready?"

I don't trust my voice yet, so I nod. I know I'll have questions to parry later.

Thorleif reaches up to a tall cupboard and pulls out a bag of metal cookie cutters. He pours them out onto the work surface with a mighty clatter.

Ingrid leans over them, expression brighter than I've seen it all night. She studies the metal cookie cutters, swiping a blonde lock off her forehead. "Is that a pig?"

I grin. "We have pigs, women, men, angels, a camel, a horse, and...." I reach for a tiny cookie cutter. "A small train."

Thorleif frowns. "Isn't there supposed to be a heart and a star as well?" He moves back to the cupboard to search for the lost shapes.

Ingrid is still digging through the pile of metal on the table, but she lights up at his words. "Right! The gingersnap hearts in the windows!"

While Thorleif rummages through the cupboards, I get the gingersnap dough out of the fridge and start slicing pieces off with a knife. The hard dough softens under my hands as the sweet scent of buttery syrup, cloves, ginger, cinnamon, and pepper wafts up to me.

Thorleif hands me a rolling pin, fingers barely brushing against mine—but somehow it's enough to make my skin tingle. This needs to stop.

I shoot him what is supposed to be a small smile, determined to shock my body into obedience. But instead of the lesson I need to learn, my gaze tangles in his—dark, and full, and steady—and I can't breathe.

His dark eyes drop to my lips and my entire body floods with heat.

Abort mission. Abort mission.

This is obviously not the way to get a hold of my wayward emotions. I drop my gaze and turn around so quickly I shave off the tip of the flour pile in the middle of the table. Thorleif coughs at the resulting cloud.

I blush. "Sorry. I didn't mean to do that." But it worked, didn't it? It totally worked.

Ingrid shakes her head. "Want me to take over rolling out that dough? You seem a bit preoccupied."

"I'm fine." I prove it by rolling the dough out to perfection, and soon, we're all grinding cookie cutters against the waxed tablecloth, and four cookie sheets are filled with angels, camels, and the lot. "I remember the year Thorleif only made pigs." I look up at Ingrid.

"We were in high school, I think, and he ended up filling a whole cookie tin with nothing but gingersnap pigs."

Ingrid rolls her eyes and turns to Thorleif. "Did you really?"

Thorleif only shrugs his broad shoulders. "Last I checked, they all taste the same."

Mor Vaage's Christmas music plays over the speaker in the other room. It's quite different from the Christmas tunes you hear on the radio here—all hymns, church organs, and chiming bells. But it does make for some hauntingly beautiful tunes.

We've baked our eighth tray of gingersnaps when the bells on the back door jingle, and a man's voice calls out a greeting.

"Olav! I didn't know you'd be here!" Thorleif brushes flour off of his apron and marches into the other room. My eyes definitely don't linger on his broad back, or the apron string tied with a bow around his waist. Not at all.

But next to me, Ingrid's back is ramrod straight. "I thought you said he wasn't going to be here!" Her whisper is sharp, but I hear the anger behind her words. The hurt?

I frown. "I didn't know he was going to be here."

What is her problem with Olav? The last time they were here together we'd have needed to soak them with water to cool down the sparking chemistry between them. But Ingrid's stiff movements and the worry on her brow tell me that won't be necessary this time. Did they have a falling out in the four days since then? When did they have time for that?

The sounds of Mor Vaage and Bestemor fussing over Olav drift in on from the living room as Thorleif re-enters the kitchen. I catch his gaze. "Did you invite him tonight?"

He shakes his head, a question in his eyes. "I didn't ask him for the *Lussekatt* baking, either, but it's not like he needs an invitation."

"Ragnhild. Can you take me home?" Ingrid wipes the flour off her hands, then unwraps the apron strings from around her waist. "I'm not feeling great."

I turn to her, gaping. "Is this about Olav?"

Ingrid's lips press together into a tight line, and she turns to hang the apron up on the line of hooks on the bathroom door. "I don't want to talk about it, Ragnhild." Her voice is quiet, but there's no question that she means business.

She washes her hands in the big kitchen sink, and dries them on a striped dish towel, all without meeting my eyes.

What the heck happened on Friday? Olav gave her a ride home so I could stay overnight at the Vaage house, but they'd seemed friendly enough when they left. Olav doesn't have the best track record when it comes to relationships, but I'm pretty sure Ingrid knows that. She did ask me if Olav would be here tonight, but I honestly didn't think he'd be. And I had no idea he'd be a deal breaker.

I brush the flour off my hands and turn to Thorleif. "I'm going to drive her home."

He nods. "Are you coming back after?"

I shake my head. "It'll be past nine by the time I make it back here, and it's getting colder. I don't really want to brave the ice."

Thorleif pulls his apron over his head. "It might be icy out there already. We can drive Ingrid home, and I'll bring you back here after. You can stay till tomorrow, right?" He hesitates, his hand going to the too-long strands of hair at the back of his neck. "Or I can drive you home, but then we'd need to find a way to get you your car tomorrow...."

He wants to drive me? The relief of not having to go back out on the road eases the tension in my shoulders but doesn't explain the warm feeling in my stomach. Or the sudden urge to run my fingers through those strands of hair he's so skillfully tugging at. An absolutely ridiculous urge.

"I can stay over. I have all my stuff in my car." Thorleif's eyes warm as they meet mine, and something melts a little in my chest. I'm not doing him a massive favor. It's not like I really have to plan for an overnight visit—I've had my toothbrush in the bathroom upstairs for years already.

I turn to Ingrid, who looks ready to walk out the door yesterday. "Is that okay for you?"

She shrugs, but her face is pale. "Sure. I just want to get home and lie down." Maybe it's not just Olav? Is she getting that awful virus that's been going around?

Olav walks into the kitchen, but as he looks around the table, his jovial expression quickly turns to a frown. "You're all leaving?"

I scowl at him. "Ingrid's got a headache, so I'm just making sure she gets well home." *Like you were supposed to do Friday.*

I have no idea what happened that night, or maybe in the days following. I wonder if he made a move, and she turned him down? It wouldn't surprise me, although it doesn't quite explain why she's so upset. She's heard enough stories about his chasing girls that this shouldn't be news to her. But something must have happened for her to be avoiding him as she is.

Olav shrugs as if he has no responsibility in the matter. "The two of you are coming back here, though, right?" He gestures to Thorleif and me while Ingrid moves past him without as much as a glance in his direction. He could be air as far as she's concerned.

"Yeah, we'll be back." Thorleif shrugs and goes to tell his mother we're leaving.

I want to talk to Olav and find out what happened with Ingrid, but although she's slinked off to the back porch, she's still within earshot. Instead of confronting him, I shove several of the coolest gingersnap cookies into a ziplock bag for her to take home.

Ingrid doesn't say much on the drive, and I can't exactly ask her what's the matter with Thorleif right there. He's my best friend, not hers, and I don't think she'd be very happy with me if I aired my suspicions. And so I stay quiet until Thorleif puts his old, green Ford in park outside her house.

She drops down from the bench seat, and I hold out the zip-lock bag of gingersnap cookies still on the seat. "Your spoils."

She smiles. "Thank you. And thanks for the invite. Sorry we had to cut it short."

I shake my head. "No worries. Please text me later, though, alright?"

She nods, and once she's safely through the door, Thorleif pulls the truck back onto the road.

It's just me and him in here, and there's a strange sort of tension in the cab with us. One that never used to be there before. It's thick and pressing against me from every side. I want to open the window to let it out, but I don't think this is the sort of thing that can be fixed by letting in some fresh air.

We drive in silence, only the loud engine and the occasional sound from Thorleif as he maneuvers the icy roads. When we finally walk through the door of the Vaage house, the jingling bells on the back door seem loud and jarring.

Once my coat and boots have found their place on the back porch, I beeline for the couch in the living room. Mor Vaage and Bestemor must have already gone to bed, because Olav is the only occupant in the cozy living room.

He looks up from his phone. "You guys are late. Are the roads that bad?"

Thorleif grimaces. "They're pretty bad. I'd probably head out if I were you."

Olav whistles, but there's a familiar twinkle in his eye. "Are you trying to get rid of me, or are they actually bad?"

"They're icy, Olav."

Olav sighs and gets up from his chair. "Alright. Good night, Ragnhild." He salutes me with a finger to his imaginary cap.

"Good night."

He frowns at my flat greeting. "What's wrong with you?"

I'm exhausted, but I pin him with the most withering glare I can muster. "I think the better question is what happened Friday night when you were supposed to take Ingrid home."

His shoulders stiffen. "Nothing happened."

But his answer is too quick, and his frown digs in a little deeper. Will I be betraying Ingrid's trust if I tell him he's the reason she wanted to go home early tonight? Probably.

"You guys spent literally all of Friday night bickering and flirting, and tonight you barely talked. Something must have happened between then and now."

Olav only shakes his head, lips pressed into a line. "It's none of your business, Ragnhild." And then he swings around to face a frowning Thorleif, cutting off any further questions I have. "I'll text you when I'm home so you can convince your mom that I'm not stranded in a ditch somewhere."

Thorleif is still frowning, but he nods. "She'll appreciate that. She's got an early shift at the hospital tomorrow."

Their conversation follows them as they walk out to the back porch, but I'm no longer paying attention. I need to talk to Ingrid—she's hurting, and I need to know why.

But not tonight. I'm too tired for that.

I'll text her tomorrow.

Sleep muddles my senses, and I close my eyes. The door slams with a sharp jingle, interrupting the soft crackle from the *Jøtul* stove. Then Olav's car starts up outside, and the sound of the engine rolls down the driveway and out onto the road.

Thorleif's footsteps sound in the living room, and I open my eyes again.

He crosses the floor, and though he hesitates, he sits down next to me as usual. He stretches his long arms over the back of the couch.

I yawn, and I hear the grin in his voice. "Long day?"

I hum my answer, and his fingers trail my shoulder farthest away from him. I don't need more convincing than that, and I lean into his warm, solid side.

The contented sigh that spills into the space between us isn't something I can control. And for a moment I'm not sure if it came from me or him.

When I wake up, I'm still snuggled up against Thorleif's shoulder. And I don't ever want to move. I snuggle closer, and his strong arm wraps even tighter around me.

I'm so warm, so comfortable I could stay here all night.

Soon a throw blanket is tucked up next to my face, and large fingers make the barest brush over my cheek. "Goodnight, Ragnhild."

CHAPTER 12

RAGNHILD

December 18th

I wake up with Thorleif's strong arms wrapped around me, snuggled into his warm shoulder that rises and falls in the rhythm of his steady breathing. The scent of laundry detergent from the fabric of his shirt and the woodsy cardamom scent I've always associated with Thorleif is almost enough to lull me back into a deep sleep. Almost.

The cold morning air seeping in from the old window panes infiltrates the still air in the room around us, and I relish the heat of his body against my side.

The fire must have petered out during the night, and I don't think the room is much warmer than the winter day outside. Not that I'd know the temperature in the room if it wasn't for that one spot where the throw slipped down from my shoulder during the night—the same throw Thorleif covered me with before I drifted off to sleep. Warmth spreads in my chest at that thought. It's hard not to admire a man whose heart is so kind.

The cold draft from the windows slips over the side of my neck making goosebumps spread across my skin. A shiver tracks across my skin, even though most of my body is warm from the giant heater I'm halfway draped over. We weren't quite this tangled up when I fell asleep, but I can't find it in my heart to be upset about it.

I know I should be.

I'm in love with Jacob, after all. He's the one I should want to be all tangled up with after falling asleep on a couch. But right now, I can't conjure up my feelings for Jacob at all.

Right now, all I want is this right here.

I want the morning that is cold and snowy, and the living room that is dark, and Thorleif who is warm and solid and safe.

I want these hazy morning moments to last.

I haven't opened my eyes yet, still hovering in that hazy space between wakefulness and sleep, where dreams that cannot be in the light are alive and well.

And I blame my next actions on that dreamy haze of early morning delirium. Because why else would I do what I know I shouldn't? Why would I want to snuggle deeper into Thorleif's embrace? Or nuzzle my nose against his warm neck?

Why would I want to taste the skin there?

I shouldn't, but I do.

Snuggle in, I mean. And maybe, just maybe that other thing, too. And maybe the way he shudders should make me regret it. Maybe the groan that sounds deep in his throat, turning my blood to fire should give me second thoughts. But they don't.

And I don't regret it.

I know it's not fair to Thorleif, even if I don't think he minds. I don't want him to realize that I know what I'm doing. That I want more of this. Of him.

Because that doesn't fit the story I've told myself for so long. It doesn't fit my need for him to stage this wedding. Because if this is how I really feel, why would I need to turn Jacob's head?

Why, when Thorleif is right here and turning his head towards me, literally and figuratively? But because I'm a coward, I quickly close my eyes, pretending I'm asleep.

His breath against my cheek is hot, and I want to open my eyes and press my mouth to his. But I only keep up my pretense, even though I'm not certain I'm fooling him.

But I really hope I do, because I don't need him to know about the war being waged inside me lately. The one where whatever tension between me and my best friend is enough to make me forget how excited I am to see Jacob tomorrow. Enough for me to fall asleep next to him without ever having the thought that I wish I was with Jacob instead.

Why am I not wishing this was Jacob?

My treacherous heart jolts as Thorleif's solid arm tightens around me, and he tugs me even closer to him. I sigh into him as he does.

New York City is so far away. And Thorleif is right here, dropping a kiss onto my forehead as if he truly believes I'm asleep. And with that kiss, my heart melts just a little more—for him, for this.

For a future I never thought I'd want.

Somehow I drift back to sleep tucked against him. When I wake up for the second time, the throw is tucked around me, but the couch is cold and Thorleif is gone.

And remembering my actions earlier this morning I have no doubt as to why he isn't here to wake me up.

I groan, rubbing a hand over my flaming face. How could I have acted like that? Sure, I was half asleep, but that's no excuse. We're putting on a fake wedding in three days, not a real one—and absolutely not a reason to act like I did. Even less so because the end goal of the wedding is a date with another man.

What is Thorleif thinking? I want to sink through the floor as embarrassment churns my stomach. I might not have regretted my actions in the moment, but God knows I regret them now! I need to find Thorleif, to apologize. I need to make this right between us.

"Good morning, Ragnhild." I startle at Bestemor Vaage's voice. Of all the people to see me like this! I chew my lip as I look up at her, but the smile she sends me is friendly enough.

But as her knowing gaze moves from my disheveled appearance to the imprint of another person on the pillows next to me, I imagine she's drawing her own conclusions as to what happened last night. And, for once, they're unlikely to be much worse than the truth.

Will my impulsivity ever bring me anything but ruined relationships?

My skin tingles with embarrassment as I press out a weak greeting in return. "Good morning, Bestemor Vaage."

Am I imagining the disapproval in her brown eyes? Probably not.

She moves on past me, and my shoulders drop their tension. Now to find Thorleif.

Once I've made sure all my clothes are covering their designated body parts, I pull the throw blanket off of me and stand up from the couch.

Maybe I should find the bathroom first. I need a shower. Or at least a toothbrush and a hot washcloth for my face. I move slowly towards the downstairs bathroom where I'm most likely to find both—and least likely to run into Thorleif.

But I'm wrong again.

Because I only move a couple of steps in the direction of the bathroom before those very steps walk me headfirst into a tall, and much too handsome, Viking.

Thorleif's hands go to my upper arms to steady me, but his eyes go wide when they meet mine. And the small hope I had that he was asleep when I kissed his neck dies a quick, agonizing death. He was definitely, definitely awake.

"You're up." His voice is still raw with sleep.

I nod, keeping my eyes firmly on his knitted wool socks.

"I'm up." My voice barely quivers, but I'm doing a lousy job of hiding my embarrassment. Thorleif knows me too well not to see right through my pretense. He'll know the truth about this morning without me needing to tell him.

There's little chance that he'll think I'm embarrassed about falling asleep with him considering how often we've done so in the past.

And so the only conclusion left to draw is that my embarrassment is from pretending I was asleep when I kissed his neck this morning.

And fine, I wasn't asleep, but saying I was in my right mind is also inaccurate. Because awake-me does not approve of asleep-me's actions. At all. And still, awake-me is the one forced to make this right again.

"You...." Thorleif clears his throat. "You sleep well?"

I nod again, maintaining eye contact with his socks.

"That's good."

Oh God, can this interaction be over soon?

Another thought occurs to me like an electric shock to my system, and my head snaps up. "Why are you not at work?"

My blood pressure ratchets up, and my vision goes dark for a moment from sheer panic. Why am *I* not at work? Shit. I'm supposed to be at the Norwegian Seamen's Church at noon. "What time is it?"

He grins at me, but it doesn't yield the comfort I'm used to at all. Have I made both of us late? After attempting to ruin our friendship?

"Relax, Ragnhild. I was just coming to wake you up. It's only 6 am. I'm not leaving for work for another half hour, and you're still on time to make it to the city."

I want to melt with relief. At least I haven't messed up too badly. But is that really true?

Thorleif turns back to the kitchen to set the table. He pulls out the breadbasket and fills it with crispbread, sliced rye, and sourdough. The homemade jams, and a charcuterie board of cheeses, smoked meat, and a cluster of grapes go next.

I plug in the triangular seven-armed candlestick in the windowsill and watch the white, electrical candles burst to life.

Mor Vaage must already be at work, because it's just Thorleif, Bestemor Vaage, and I at the table. Am I imagining Bestemor Vaage's disapproving attention on the diminished space between Thorleif and me on the bench? Maybe. Or maybe I'm not.

Unease scrambles my stomach, and I struggle to finish my half slice of sourdough with raspberry jam. What if Thorleif figures out that I was awake?

And if he doesn't, I still need to figure out why I did what I did. Especially because Thorleif is not the man I have a crush on.

I'm supposed to be with Jacob.

Am I not?

My heart sinks as Thorleif's eyes never quite meet mine as we pass each other on our trips through the house; emptying the table, putting the dishes in the sink, and getting ready to leave.

When I walk outside, the bitter cold air takes my breath away. Thorleif shuts the door behind us and walks over to his truck. He'll let the diesel engine warm up for a few minutes, so I'll be out of here before him. But will this cloud of awkwardness follow me home?

I say a quick goodbye without meeting his eyes.

But when I get into my chilled car and turn the key, the engine only lets out a disinterested rumble. I try again, but it still doesn't turn over. Why? Of all days does my car need to act up today?

Thorleif is at my window. "Let me try it."

I get out of the car and Thorleif folds his giant frame into the driver's seat. But he's not successful either.

I want to cry. I don't have that much extra time if I want to make it down to the city in time for my shift.

"I'll give you a jump. Just let me get my truck turned around. Why don't you go in the house? It's freezing out here." Normally I'd find it sweet that he'd want me to be warm, but today I'm not so sure he's not just trying to get rid of me.

"Okay." I trudge back inside to an empty living room, but I'm not alone long. Thorleif comes back inside, rubbing his hands and blowing into them. "I'll just let it sit for a bit and it should start right up."

"Aren't you a mechanic, don't you have a cheat code?"

He rolls his eyes. "That is the cheat code."

And he's right of course, the car starts right up when we get back outside. And because he's Thorleif, he insists on following me back to my apartment and makes me promise to keep the car running while I run inside and grab my stuff.

But his lack of conversation while we waited for my car to start makes me wonder if I've been wrong all this time.

If I didn't feel anything for him, would I have done what I did this morning? And would it make me feel as rotten keeping the full story from him?

I step out of my car, dutifully keeping the engine running. Thorleif rolls down his window while I step gingerly across the frozen driveway. "Thank you. I'll see you later."

Thorleif nods, but his eyes are on his hand messing with the radio. Each crackle from the speakers is another arrow into my heart.

"Have a good day at work, Ranghild." But his voice is strained, and he doesn't look up even once as he rolls up the window.

As I quickly change my clothes and grab my things in the house, I no longer wonder *if* I've messed up—just how badly.

And whether or not this damage is something I can possibly fix.

CHAPTER 13

THORLEIF

Holding Ragnhild in my arms while she sleeps is further than I thought I'd ever get with her. Sure, we've fallen asleep together hundreds of times—after a late-night movie, studying together, or even just during our many sleepovers as kids. But this is different. This—holding her against me while her body is soft and warm against mine, her even breathing hot against my neck—feels nothing like any other time I can remember.

My chest warms at the thought that she trusts me enough to fall asleep with me. I think I knew that she would, but it's not something I take for granted.

The fire in the *Jøtul* stove has flickered out during the night, and the chill from outside is creeping in through the walls and the single-paned windows. I really should get up and start the fire before the room gets too cold, but I'm worried that if I move I'll wake Ragnhild. And while there is a chance she'll just turn around and go back to sleep, there's also the chance that she'll freak out. That she'll scramble up from the couch the way she did the last time we were this close, during that tickle fight on Saturday.

I know I haven't done a great job of hiding my attraction to her lately, and I don't regret that. But I'm fully aware that she's mostly responded by becoming more skittish. Which doesn't bode well for the fact that I'm more comfortable right now than I've been in a long time.

My head and right shoulder might be significantly colder than I like, but all the parts of me that have Ragnhild snuggled up to them are nice and toasty. And I don't dare move. I'm happy to suffer frostbite on one side of my body if it means I can keep holding her.

She stirs in her sleep, and I hold my breath. But she doesn't wake up, and my heart rate slows back down.

I know I can't inspire her to fall in love with me. She's either attracted to me, or she's not. And if she isn't, there isn't a force in the world that will make her so. No matter how many best friends to lovers romance novels I sneak into her stash of books in the backroom.

The problem is that I think she *is* attracted to me. There's no way I'm imagining the charged air between us, or the way she watches me when she thinks I'm not looking. I've loved this girl for a very long time, and it feels like I've waited a lifetime for her to return those feelings. And now that I think she finally is, we're caught up in pretending to get married—as if we're just another one of the couples in the books she loves.

Ragnhild snuggles closer, and my pulse kicks up another notch. When she nuzzles her nose against my neck, my breath catches in my throat, and I shudder. She's asleep, right? She has to be. I hold very still, and her face stays pressed to my neck, then….

Holy heck, is she…. Did she just *lick* my neck? I can't help the groan that slips out. All fears of startling her forgotten, I turn towards her, wanting to catch her lips with mine.

But her eyes are closed and her breathing even. My skin is on fire, but I hold still and watch for a flicker of her eyelashes, a smile sliding over her lips, any sign that she is awake right now. But there's nothing. She's really asleep.

I tighten my arm around her, tucking her even closer as I stare into the faint light from the snow outside. I drop a kiss onto her forehead, but she doesn't stir. But no matter how much I try, I can't find the same peace she has. I can't go back to sleep.

My blood is still running hot through my veins from her open-mouthed kisses on my throat. My mind keeps conjuring up where they could have led if she'd done it on purpose. As it is, it seems she had no idea what she was doing. And it's disappointing as hell.

Was she even aware that it was me she kissed? What if she was having a dream about another man, and I was just the physical stand-in? What if her dream was about Jacob?

My stomach roils, and I feel sick.

I no longer feel content holding her against me while one side of my body slowly turns to ice. I need to get up and go for a long walk. It doesn't matter that my alarm is likely an hour or more away from going off, or that the achy feeling in my bones tells me I need more sleep. I need space more.

I wait for what feels like forever, but when I get up it's still only 4 am, and I have two whole hours before I'm supposed to get up.

I start the coffee, take a shower, drink the coffee, get dressed, and still it's only 4.38 am. I open the *Jøtul* stove and blow on the coals until they catch onto the ripped newspaper and bundle of twigs in my hand. Then I watch while the fire takes hold of the firewood while Ragnhild snores in the background. Even after that, the clock is no more than 5 am.

Bestemor comes downstairs, and we enjoy another cup of coffee together in the stillness of the living room. I'm not even afraid to wake up Ragnhild at this point, but the rocking chairs by the doors are far enough away she won't feel awkward if she does happen to wake up.

"You two never went to bed last night, did you?" Bestemor's eyes are much too awake for an 85-year-old who's woken up from a long night of sleep. And far too knowing for it to be a question.

I still answer it, my cheeks hot with embarrassment. "No, we did not."

She smiles into her coffee, and I'm surprised by her reaction. I thought she might discourage me from spending any more time with Ragnhild after her wild article, but that is not the vibe I'm getting at all. If anything, Bestemor seems like she's enjoying this news of us falling asleep together on the couch. As if she hopes it's the start of something new.

Maybe things aren't forever messed up between her and Ragnhild?

An hour later, my alarm goes off on my phone, and I go to wake Ragnhild. I get no farther than the kitchen doorway before she walks into me. She lets out a gasp as I catch her upper arms to steady her.

She must have just woken up because she still appears half asleep.

My skin burns as I remember her nuzzling her face against my neck. If she wasn't awake she wouldn't remember it, would she? I need to tell her, but how do I bring it up?

Or would it be kinder to keep it to myself? I could just let her think that we fell asleep on the couch, I woke up and got up before her, and that was the extent of it. I swallow, trying to judge my next steps. "You're up."

Her gaze drops from mine to my feet, and she nods. "I'm up."

Her embarrassment confuses me. Is she embarrassed that she fell asleep here? No, that makes no sense. My heart pounds. The only thing she could possibly be embarrassed about was if she was awake during that kiss. If she kissed me on purpose. Did she?

I rub the back of my neck, not quite knowing how to process

this information. "You...." I clear my throat of the remnants of sleep, but it still sounds scratchy. "You sleep well?" She nods, still not meeting my eyes. I've known her too long not to read into that.

Her expression is the same one she had when she was eight and tried to pretend she didn't eat the rice crispy bars left over after Halloween. Except, this is far more serious than rice crispy bars, and there's a lot more than leftover Halloween candy on the line.

I nod slowly. "That's good."

But it's not good. Because I know now that she wasn't asleep. She kissed me, and she wasn't asleep when it happened. Which means she knew it was me. She didn't think it was Jacob she was kissing. She knew it was me all along.

And...was she not going to tell me?

Her head suddenly snaps up. "Why are you not at work? What time is it?" Wild panic shines in her eyes, and I forget my own spiraling thoughts for a moment.

I grin and shake my head. There's no reason for her to be so freaked out. "Relax, Ragnhild. I was just coming to wake you up. It's only 6 am. I haven't left for work yet, and you're still on time to make it to the city."

Her shoulders drop, and her eyes fall closed. When they open, they only meet mine for a second. A shuttered second.

Does she know that I know?

There's no time to talk while I set the table and make more coffee. We sit down to eat with Bestemor, making quick work of lighting the candles and singing. We clear the table and make it to the back porch at the same time. When we walk outside in the bitter cold morning, Ragnhild walks to start her car, while I swing myself up into the driver's seat of my truck and start warming the glow plugs. After three rounds, I turn the engine and it roars to life.

Loud as it is, I can't help but notice that there are no sounds of an engine starting from Ragnhild's car. Just Ragnhild's expression growing more and more frustrated through the windshield.

Leaving the engine running, I drop to the ground and jog over to her.

She cranks it one more time, but it doesn't turn over.

"Let me try it."

She gets out and lets me give it a shot, but I have no more luck than she did. Ragnhild's shoulders shake as she wraps her arms around herself, eyes a little too shiny, as if she's on the verge of crying.

I tilt my head in the direction of the house. "I'll give you a jump. Just let me get my truck turned around. Why don't you go in the house? It's freezing out here."

After hooking up the cables, I follow her inside. I can barely feel my hands as I rub them together. I drop down into the unoccupied rocking chair by the window. "I'll just let it sit for a bit and it should start right up."

She frowns. "Aren't you a mechanic, don't you have a cheat code?"

I roll my eyes. "That is the cheat code."

The living room is quiet as we wait, but I have no words to fill the silence. No matter how many questions are burning at the back of my mind, now isn't the time to ask them.

When I go back outside, the car starts right back up. I still insist on following her home, and make sure to tell her that she can't turn it off until she's at her final destination.

I pull my truck in behind the other car in Ragnhild's driveway. I roll down my window and fresh winter air blows into the cab from outside. I fiddle with the radio, trying to find a station without Christmas music, watching her move across the slippery driveway out of the corner of my eye.

"See you later." Her voice is flat, and I nod in response.

"Have a good day at work, Ragnhild." I pull my truck back out, turning it around. I watch her wave in my rear-view mirror, and I hate the dejection on her face, in her hunched shoulders. But I also don't know exactly what to do with the fact that she likes me more than she's let on.

And that she's keeping it a secret.

Did she just realize it, or has she known the whole time? And is seeing where this attraction will lead us really worth it if it wrecks our friendship?

CHAPTER 14

RAGNHILD

December 19th

"We should make a station where the kids can fish candy bags from behind a sheet. Did you ever do that as a child?" Jacob's question comes from far away.

The silence following it never fills with my answer. Instead, Jacob lets out a deep chuckle. One that normally turns my stomach into a gooey mess—just not today. He taps his fingers on the table of the meeting room at the Seamen's Church where we've sat for the last hour. "Ragnhild? Did you get enough sleep last night? You look exhausted."

I shift in the padded, red chair and frown at his ridiculously handsome face as I try to remember what we were discussing. "Yeah." I push out a weak smile. "Definitely not enough sleep." I straighten in my seat, grip the pencil to poise it over my pitifully empty notepad, and try to focus on the task at hand.

Normally, getting to spend an entire work shift with Jacob would have me in a haze of bliss. But even though we've spent the last hour brainstorming children's games for the upcoming Christmas tree party, the knot that formed in my stomach yesterday still hasn't dissolved.

Am I making a mistake with this fake wedding? I can't call it off two days before, can I? I meet Jacob's gaze. His warm eyes are blue with golden flecks—mesmerizing on any other day. But I'm so worried about the distance I sense between Thorleif and me that his gaze doesn't have the usual effect.

I texted Thorleif before I went to bed, and while he answered, his text was short and to the point. And I hate it.

I was hoping a good night's sleep would make me feel better, but instead of sleeping, I tossed and turned and replayed the events of the morning—again and again until I could no longer bear to stay in bed.

Today has been just as miserable as yesterday but with the added lack of sleep. I can't laugh at Jacob's jokes the way I normally do. Not when Thorleif won't be there to stoically resist laughing at mine when I get home.

When I step off the subway car onto the platform and walk away from the pressing mass of New York City, I feel none of the usual relief. Driving home, I'm still kicking myself for not telling Thorleif the truth before he figured it out on his own. I don't hear a word of my audiobook, and halfway home, I turn it off.

I don't know what came over me yesterday morning, or how I could act that way when there's never been anything romantic between us. I'm still struggling to understand that part, but that's no excuse for not telling him I was awake. I need to talk to him, to clear the air between us.

But when I finally arrive at the Vaage house, Thorleif's truck isn't parked in the driveway. Is he not home from work yet?

For a second, my courage fails me, and I consider turning back home. I could just go back to my empty apartment. I could text him and ask if we can talk tomorrow.

No. I need to talk to him tonight. If I wait, I'm going to chicken out.

I turn up the driveway and park my car. I push the door open and move as quickly as I can through the darkness, which isn't very fast since I'm also trying to avoid slipping on the ice and breaking my neck.

The bells on the back door let off their cheerful jingle as I leave the sullen December darkness behind. When I enter the living room, the fire in the *Jøtul* stove snaps and crackles as Mor Vaage places another log into its hungry belly.

Soft guitar notes and Alf Prøysen's soothing voice stream into the room from the speaker in the corner, bringing me back to every December night I've spent at this house.

Mor Vaage looks up from where she's kneeling on the floor by the *Jøtul* stove. "Hi Ragnhild, how was work?"

I shrug and force a smile, but I can tell she's not fooled in the slightest. Just like Thorleif wouldn't be.

Mor Vaage pushes up from the floor and brushes the sawdust off her clothes. "Would you like some coffee? I just made some, and we have more *julemenn* cookies than we'll be able to eat before New Year's."

I hesitate. I should wait for Thorleif. He is the one I need to speak with. But maybe getting an outsider's perspective will be good, too. Mor Vaage isn't exactly a neutral third party, but I don't know who else I'd ask for advice. Ingrid is still acting distant, my mother is no longer in my life, and it's not like I can ask anyone at work when they all think I'm about to get married. I bite my lip. "Yes, I'd love some coffee."

She smiles that smile that feels like home, with eyes that see too much. Her gaze lingers on the dark shadows under my eyes, and I doubt my smile looks as real as I want it to. Soon we're both seated at the farmhouse table, a plate of *julemenn* and two steaming mugs of coffee between us.

"Are things not well between you and Thorleif?" Mor Vaage

certainly doesn't dance around the real reason I'm here.

I clutch my cup of coffee tighter, glancing towards the blanket separating this room from the backroom. But I've heard no truck in the driveway, so Thorleif can't possibly be there to overhear me.

Mor Vaage follows my gaze. "He said he might be late today, and that maybe he'd stop by Olav's."

I nod and decide to go for it. "I did something stupid."

I have no plans to tell this kind woman the details of what happened. That's more information than she needs or likely wants. But I do need to tell her *something*, and the gist of it is that I made a mistake and made things weird between Thorleif and me.

"We all do stupid things from time to time." Mor Vaage bites into a white, pillowy *julemann* cookie from the plate on the kitchen table. I'm quite certain I do stupider things more often than she does, but I'm not going to argue.

"I really like this guy at my work."

She nods, but her blue eyes give nothing away. "And you did something to offend him?"

I shake my head. "No, everything is fine with us. We have tons of chemistry, and I think he likes me, too. But I did something stupid to Thorleif, and I didn't tell him. And then he found out, and we haven't really talked since."

She chews her cookie, a thoughtful expression on her face. "Was this stupid thing related to the guy you work with?"

I shake my head. "Not directly, but I think I gave Thorleif the wrong idea about it."

She hums and takes another sip of coffee. "So apart from the chemistry, what do you like about this guy?"

I sip my coffee, buying time to figure out my answer. "We go well together; work well together. He's good with kids."

Her eyes are so impossibly blue, and her question pierces me in its honesty. "Is that enough to build a life on? A relationship?"

Is it? "I don't know." I shrug and push the thought away, because

I'm not here to talk about Jacob. I'm here to talk to Thorleif and beg his forgiveness. If he'll let me.

She smiles. "I'm sorry things are strained between you and Thorleif. I hope you'll work it out." She empties her mug. "I think the two of you are good together."

My eyes go wide and my cheeks hot. "As a couple?"

She laughs, probably at the disbelief in my voice. "No, just in general."

My face feels even hotter. "Good. Because I think Jacob and I are perfect for each other."

She nods. "The guy at work?"

"Yes." But I don't look at her. My full attention is on the blanket hanging between the back porch and the living room. And on the man who pushes it aside as he enters the room. I didn't even hear his truck.

My heart aches as he straightens. And I want to cry at the tension sneaking into his shoulders when his searching eyes see me. "Ragnhild? Are you okay? Why are you here?"

I shake my head, because I'm going to cry if I try to speak.

Mor Vaage saves me. "I think she's here to talk to you. We're just done with our coffee, but maybe you can make another batch, and you two can talk?"

Thorleif raises an eyebrow at me. "Does that sound okay?"

I nod, swallowing down my tears. "Yeah."

I try to compose myself while Thorleif makes coffee and brings out another stack of *julemenn*. They are my favorite, but my stomach is too full of nerves for me to take as much of a bite. He tops off my coffee, then pours the rest into his mug, and sits down on the bench next to me. One long leg on either side of the bench and coffee in hand, he pins me with his dark gaze. "Alright, spill."

Shit. I can't do this. There's no way I can tell him that I kissed him and pretended I was asleep. I'm going to combust from embarrassment.

"Ragnhild?" His voice is serious. "Is everything alright? Are you sick?"

I shake my head, pulling in a deep breath, and bracing myself for whatever will happen next. "We need to talk about yesterday morning."

"Oh." His mug thuds down on the table.

I can't even look at him. "I was sort of awake. And then when I actually woke up I was so embarrassed. And then you found out, and now you're mad at me. And I hate the distance between us, and you're not answering my texts and—"

He cuts me off. "I've been answering your texts, Ragnhild."

I shake my head, daring a glance at him. "Not like normal. You've been short. It's been weird."

He frowns. "I can maybe see that they've been shorter than usual, but I'm not mad at you."

It's my turn to frown as I search his handsome face. No, not handsome, just…. Just Thorleif-like. "You're not? Why are you not mad at me?"

He laughs and lifts his coffee to his lips again. "Are you seriously complaining that I'm not mad at you?"

I roll my eyes. "No. I'm relieved. And, just for the record, asleep-me was not acting with my permission, and I'm sorry if it gave you the wrong idea."

"Uh-huh." His eyes are too full of laughter, and my face is burning again. "I'm sure you are."

I punch him playfully in the stomach, and he groans, doubling over. "Was this also done without your permission?"

I groan. He's never going to let me live that down. Never. "No, that was with my full permission, and I'll do it again."

He straightens and grabs the rest of the *julemenn* on the plate. "Alright. I'm going to go find my book. Unless asleep-you have anything else on the agenda?" That last sentence has all the mischief dancing in his eyes, and he's going to be the death of me.

I bury my face in my hands, my voice muffled between my fingers. "No, nothing."

"Right, then." And he walks off, laughing. And as I'm staring after his broad back I don't know if I should be happy he's joking around with me again, or worried at how easily he's taking this in stride.

I do know that I can't wait for our pretend wedding day to be in the past. Maybe then I'll feel less confused.

CHAPTER 15

RAGNHILD

December 20th

Ingrid plops down onto the couch in my living room. She might as well have lived in Antarctica for as difficult as it's been to get her to come over to my apartment. In reality, she lives just ten minutes away.

It's the downside to living upstate, I suppose, everything is miles away from everything else, requiring a twenty-minute drive to get anywhere. But it also allows for snowy, sun-dappled fields in the mornings, and night skies with so many more stars than you'll ever see in town.

And the bone-chilling howls of coyotes. I shudder.

But I have Ingrid here now, at last, lured out from her own dingy abode with the promise of the batch of fresh baked *julemenn* and bottle of *gløgg* Mor Vaage sent me home with yesterday. *Gløgg* is hard enough to come by that it's like kryptonite for those of us who've wrapped our hands around a cupful of it on a cold winter night—stomping our feet in the snow to keep warm, and after every sip, let our sweet, spicy breaths fog up the velvety darkness.

I chop almonds and drop them into the mugs before pouring the hot spicy drink over the mixture. When I hand my other best friend her steaming mug, she wraps her fingers around it as if she's desperate for the comfort. And judging by the shadows under her eyes, that's not far from the truth.

I perch on the armrest with my own steaming mug of Norwegian winter comfort. "Ingrid. What happened last Friday?"

She pulls in a sip, wincing at the burn on her tongue, not quite meeting my eyes. "Is that why you asked me over?"

I roll my eyes and take a sip from the mug. It burns my tongue, too. "Are you surprised at that?"

Her shoulders sag, and she shakes her head. "No. And it's not that I don't want to talk to you. I just haven't even sorted it out in my mind."

I feel a sting of guilt. If there's something I understand, it's this. I've tried to sort out my relationships with Thorleif and Jacob for a week and a half. And even though my wedding—fake wedding—is tomorrow, I am no closer to knowing exactly what to do.

I can't cancel the wedding. And I don't want to. Jacob is still as handsome and kind and perfect as he was at the beginning of the week, and I know all he needs is a nudge.

And he'll have it.

But Thorleif? Thorleif has feelings for me that are stronger than I realized. And in light of our sudden chemistry, that is concerning. I push out a long breath.

A smile pulls at Ingrid's lips, and her eyes dance. It seems like forever since I've seen her like this. "Do *you* need to talk about anything, Ragnhild? Or anyone?" Her eyebrows rise.

I laugh and shake my head. "Maybe. But you first."

She pulls in a deep breath, steeling herself for the conversation. "Okay. I just. I really liked Olav. I mean, I do like him."

Alarm bells clang in my stomach. "Ingrid…"

She shakes her head, and her eyes turn shiny. "I know he's not a relationship type. I guess I just hoped it would be different?" Her last words are almost a sob.

I jump down from my perch, put both our mugs on the coffee table, and wrap my arms around her. "He turned you down?"

She stiffens, hesitating, but then she melts into my hug. "Pretty much."

I shake my head and pull her tighter. "You're incredible, Ingrid. I don't know why he can't see that. Judging by the other night, I thought he was into you."

She laughs, a harsh sound that holds no joy. "Well, he was that. Just not interested in a relationship." God, I hate him. Hate him for hurting her, for not seeing all she is and could be.

"I'm sorry, Ingrid. Your body is the least interesting thing about you."

Ingrid lets out another sob against my shoulder. "I know…." She sniffs and pulls in a deep breath. Another sniff sounds as she tries to gain her composure. "I know he's fully within his right not to want more, but…. I just hoped we could, you know?"

"I get that." I rub her back, wishing there was more I could do. Wishing that my friend being beautiful, smart, and kind would be enough for Olav to be interested in a relationship with her— knowing it isn't.

Ingrid pulls out of my embrace, wipes her palms against her wet cheeks, and straightens. "I don't want to talk more about it. Let's talk about you instead."

I sit back, reach for my cup of *gløgg*, suspecting I'll need the fortification. "What about me?"

She laughs. "Right. Um… You know how lots of people can have their aprons tied by another person without literally falling apart?"

My cheeks heat. I can still feel Thorleif's hands brushing against my back three days later, which is as ridiculous as the fact that it made my skin tingle in the first place. "I have no idea what you're talking about."

Ingrid sips her *gløgg*, no more fooled by that statement than Mor Vaage would be. "Of course you don't. You're still into Jacob, right? So what's going on between you and Thorleif?"

I shake my head. "Nothing." Because it's the truth, isn't it? "There's nothing going on between us."

She frowns. "Do you want there to be something?"

"No." I shake my head because I don't want that. Of course, I don't want that.

Ingrid bites her lip, but it doesn't keep her mischievous smile from slipping out. "Then why are we even having this conversation, Ragnhild? Why did your breath catch and your face turn red when he tied your apron on Tuesday?"

I squirm under her scrutiny because I have no good answer to that. All I know is that I have a fake wedding to stage tomorrow and that I can't pull out. Not now. Not when it's so close. Nor do I want to.

Ingrid takes one more sip of her drink and pins me with her blue eyes. "If you have a crush on Jacob, why are there so many sparks between you and Thorleif?"

Why, indeed?

CHAPTER 16

RAGNHILD

December 21st, Solsnu (winter solstice)

S aturday morning arrives with nausea so strong I'm a quarter inch away from canceling the entire fake wedding. I type out a text to Thorleif, telling him I'm sick and can't go through with it.

But I can't do it. I can't cancel.

I have to do this. Jacob and I are a perfect match, and I know if I pull out now, I'll regret it forever. I delete the text and send my customary "good morning" text instead.

Thorleif: Morning. I'm outside.

Ragnhild: What? I'm still in bed.

Thorleif: Did you look at the time? Do I need to come up there and pull you out from under the covers?

My stomach does a tiny little somersault at the thought of Thorleif in my bedroom. Which is completely irrational seeing as he's been here plenty. We've even had sleepovers here, though any actual sleeping *he* did happened on my couch in the other room. But we've watched movies together in this bed, and he's helped me strip the sheets off to shake out the popcorn crumbs before I could sleep. Why didn't those movie nights incite somersaults?

I send him an eye roll emoji, ignoring the tightening in my belly. Thorleif is my best friend, this is *normal chemistry between adults of the opposite sex* stuff—nothing else!

But the feeling doesn't go away while I brush my teeth, pull a brush through my wild hair, and pull on my jeans and a cute sweater.

It gets worse.

My phone beeps with another text.

Thorleif: Seriously, I'm coming up there.

There's a flicker in my chest. What's with the bodily reactions? This is ridiculous. Standing in front of the full-length mirror on the back of my door, I survey my outfit. Tight jeans and a white cashmere wool sweater with a sparkling blue and pink butterfly across the chest. It's an expensive sweater I'd normally never splurge on, but I found it in a thrift store for less than the price of a large coffee, and I have no complaints.

I'll be wearing my Norwegian national costume, my *bunad*, for the ceremony, but on the off chance I run into Jacob before I get changed, I want to look as cute as possible. And this outfit definitely fits the bill.

I grab the garment bag with my national costume and shove my make-up bag into my purse. It's 6 am already. I don't have time to do my make-up here, but surely I can fit it into the four hours it will take us to drive down to the city?

But I feel no more certain of my big plan when my make-up is done and we stand crammed together like sardines inside a subway car.

When the car rocks to a halt, another swarm of people pours in through the open doors. Nausea swims in my stomach, and my knees are about as supportive as jelly. I tighten my grip on Thorleif's hand. His other arm wraps around my back, and as much as I don't want to, I lean into it. I don't have much of a choice if I want to remain upright.

"You okay?" The deep timbre of his voice in my ear does nothing to calm the raging storm in my stomach—but everything to raise my heart rate. His arm around me shouldn't feel this good, shouldn't make me want to tuck closer to him. But it does, and I do.

His full beard tickles my cheek, and his breath warms my ear, making me tremble. I'm much too aware that his broad chest is sheltering me from the onslaught of strangers—too aware that it's always been like this with him. Too aware that Thorleif has always sheltered me. Literally and figuratively.

"I'm okay." I push out a trembling breath. "Not good with crowds."

"You don't say." The chuckle that rumbles through his chest settles my frayed nerves. How often have I heard that sound through the years? How often have I let it assure me that all is well? That rumble is the sound of long conversations on the wood pile. Of summer nights by the Vaage's pond. It's the sound of home. *Keep your eye on the prize, Ragnhild. Thorleif isn't the man for you.*

I pull in another unsteady breath and lean away from Thorleif's chest.

Suddenly, I need distance—need to not breathe in that intoxicating aroma that always follows him. Woodsmoke, cardamom, and something else I can't place but that wreaks havoc on my logic. Based on how it makes my heart flutter uncomfortably in my chest, whatever scent it is should cost a lot more than Thorleif's sense of frugality will have let him spend at the drugstore. "I think I'm fine now."

"If you say so. Your face is a bit green." His brows dip over his dark eyes, and he looks anything but convinced. He's right, of course, but right now, I really need him to *not* be right.

I have to be fine.

I have put way too much into this plan to get cold feet and pull out at the last minute.

I lock my eyes on the shiny pole bursting from the floor of the subway car and try not to squirm under his searching gaze. "I'm fine, Thorleif."

"Wedding jitters?" Is that...*humor* in his voice? I lift my head in disbelief, and sure enough, the tilt of his lips matches the glint in those dark eyes. Irritation blooms in my chest. There's nothing funny about the lengths I'm needing to go to to get Jacob to ask me out.

"If the wedding is a fake, the jitters should be too, right?" I say it as much for my benefit as for his. I need to get it together.

Thorleif's eyes narrow, darken as he holds my gaze. "I've known you since you were in diapers, Ragnhild. You're not faking it with me."

I bristle, and defensiveness slips into my voice. "You don't know *everything* about me." Why am I picking a fight with him? He's giving up a lot for me to be here today.

Thorleif regards me for a moment, brow furrowed. "You're right. I *don't* know this Jacob, or what he did to deserve both your single-minded attention and my Saturday off work."

Heat rushes into my cheeks, both at what I'm making Thorleif do and at the thought of Jacob. What will he say when he sees me ready to get married? If I run into him before the ceremony, will we even need to go through with it? An exasperated sigh slips out before I can reel it in. "Jacob and I are meant to be. And you're not doing this for him—you're doing it for me."

The truth of my words hits me like a brick to the head. To my heart.

Thorleif is here because of me, of course, he is. Because he feels a lot more for me than the brotherly love I need him to. And instead of respecting that, as a decent person would, I'm using his feelings for me to turn the head of another guy. Despicable doesn't begin to describe it.

Remorse rushes into my chest, threatening to choke me. Some best friend I am.

"Thorleif?" I keep my gaze on an exhausted woman clutching the handle of a stroller in the seat behind him.

He shifts. "Yeah?"

I can't meet his eyes. Instead, I follow the movements of the woman behind him as she digs in her purse. A second later she pulls out a pacifier. The baby in the stroller lets out a pitiful little wail. I'm right there with him. "You know you don't have to do this. I hate that you feel like—"

He cuts me off. "And you know how I feel, how?" I wilt completely under the sharp voice he rarely, if ever, directs at me. When I move my gaze to his face, his eyes burn with emotion, and guilt pierces me.

"I don't. I…. You're right. I don't know how you feel." I study his leather boots, and an odd desire to see those sturdy boots march towards home while his strong arms carry me out of here, rises up in me.

But his strong arms do nothing but pull taut the fabric of his button-down shirt as he folds them across his chest. "You still want to go through with this, right?" His gaze searches mine, and I wish I could let him see the confusion swirling up in me. Or maybe he can.

I bite my lip. I'm sure he wants me to say no. He must know that this is as far beyond my comfort zone as I've ever ventured. But I can't tell him how I really feel—I've worked too hard to concoct this plan. "Of course, I want to go through with it."

Jacob and I have chemistry like nobody's business. The glances he sends me when I pass him in the carpeted hallways are never creepy but—boy howdy, do I want to fan myself just at the thought of them!

But is chemistry enough to build a life on? What do you know of him apart from that? The voice in my head sounds a lot like Mor Vaage's. But then it *would* be her voice. I'm certain she'd rather I dated her son than the coworker she's never met. I push her wisdom down deep, along with the rest of the avalanche of doubts her son's earnest gaze is setting off.

Jacob is great with kids. Jacob volunteers weekly at the soup kitchen. Jacob turns my knees into jelly.

I glance at the garment bags slung over Thorleif's arm, wipe my slick palms on my jeans, and focus my mind on the logistics of my plan. We should have enough time to change into our national costumes before the ceremony, even with the extensive lines we endured getting onto this crowded metal box. Did we put enough money in the parking meter for Thorleif's truck to last us till we get back?

But as doggedly as I guide my frantic thoughts, they jump back to where I don't want them all the same. Is this really the only way to get Jacob's attention? Will it work?

My heart races behind my ribcage, and my palms feel clammy again. I wipe them in the same spot on my jeans again, hoping nobody is secretly watching and guessing at my internal panic.

But as I glance around me, my eyes catch on the knowing gaze of my best friend. The friend who hasn't missed a thing. The one who's talked me through an anxiety attack more than once. I drop my gaze quicker than the temperature drops after dark, feeling like a complete fool.

It will work. I know it will. Jacob likes me, I'm sure of it. All he needs is a little nudge, and what better nudge than seeing the woman of your dreams walk down the aisle toward another man? Especially a man like Thorleif, whose tall stature and broad shoulders have turned the heads of more than one woman, and a few men, since we got to the city.

My train of thought is cut short as the subway car creaks to a halt. Before the doors open, ready to spit us out onto the platform, I sneak a glance at Thorleif—and I'm not the only one.

Yeah, Jacob will be jealous alright.

Thorleif catches my gaze, the question from earlier still in his eyes. I know if I tell him I've changed my mind, he'll take me right back to his truck, and the farm, and never say another word about my ridiculous plan. He'll have my back. He's always had my back.

My stomach churns, for more than one reason, but I nod again. "I want to do this."

His jaw sets, but he dips his head. Then the doors open with a rush of air, and the throng of humans move like a great wave. Pulling us out onto the platform. Pushing us towards the stairs—like a maelstrom aiding us up into the city that never sleeps.

The crisp, filthy air hits my lungs like ice water. The noise of traffic merges with the masses of people until it's a rumbling monster threatening to crush me. The city sways from side to side in front of me. Struggling to keep from hurling, I rally my strength.

I can do this. I have to do this.

Thorleif's hand presses against the small of my back, but the effect is more like having white hot coals pressed to my skin. I pull in a sharp breath as fire snakes its way through my veins, heats my blood, and flushes my skin. And for a nanosecond, all I want is to lean into his touch, into him.

And then my senses return. Because I'm here to catch the eye of a man, but not this one. His hand is still on my back, and I all but arch away from his touch.

"What are you doing?" I hiss the words, pushing the trail of desire far, far down. Next to the stupid doubts, the imposter syndrome that's been choking me since this morning, and Mor Vaage's sage wisdom.

"I'm playing the part." He whispers the words into my hair, his breath as warm as the steady arm he wraps around my shoulders. "Also, you look like you're about to pass out. Your face was really pale earlier, and now it's flushed."

My cheeks burn even hotter. Doesn't he understand that his touching me like this doesn't help the flush, or the lightheadedness? His face is so close to mine—his whisper so much louder than the raging noise of the city around us. Big cities are not my scene. I don't think it's ever been my scene.

I wish with a desperation that claws at my nerves that we were back on the farm. Instead of being stuck in this sickening crowd, I could curl up on the couch next to him. Let the calm rise and fall of his chest steady me. Let the crackle from the *Jøtul* stove and the turning of each page in the book he'd be reading lull me to sleep.

But I can't do any of that. Because I've chosen to pull us both away from all of that and into this stuffy cluster of skyscrapers slowly squeezing all the courage from my lungs.

Knees weak, I lean into the arm holding me as anxiety and embarrassment wage war within me. Can I really do this? Can I go through with a fake wedding when Thorleif will be there the whole time, looking at me like he is?

My heart sinks, because I know the answer to that.

Not with his dark eyes warm on mine, I can't.

CHAPTER 17

THORLEIF

I prop my hand flat against the cold glass door of the building of the Norwegian Seamen's Church, holding it open so Ragnhild can step under my arm and into the large foyer. She halts as soon as she crosses the threshold, her shoulders shrinking just a little more into her winter coat. Her words on the subway may have sounded confident, but her body language both then and now screams uncertainty.

I've spent the whole trip here kicking myself for not doing more to deter her from this plan. I don't think it will work, or at least not as smoothly as I imagine Ragnhild thinks it will. I may have fallen in love with my best friend, much like seventy-five percent of the main characters in said best friend's stash of romance novels, but real life isn't that easy—or as romantic. My current predicament should be proof enough of that.

Ragnhild sways, still frozen on the threshold of the building. I wrap my arm around her shoulders and push her farther into the room. Enough for the door to shut out the noisy city behind us. Once we're fully inside, warm, dry air envelopes us. Cheery Christmas music plays from speakers in the corners, and green garlands with tiny Norwegian flags are strung across the lobby. My eyes are immediately drawn to the large, fully decorated, Christmas tree next to the receptionist's desk. We're only three days away from Christmas Eve, and I dare say that whoever canceled their wedding last minute is having a much worse weekend than me.

I glance back down at the girl by my side. Her color is still too green for my liking. I wish she'd lay this ridiculous plan to rest, and let me whisk her away out of here. We could be back on the farm in a couple of hours, eat dinner together, and forget all about this trip. And I can forget about the fact that the girl I love is trying to win another man's heart, and figure out how I'll go about winning hers.

And I will find a way to win it. I'm not here because I believe in her plan. I'm only here because I can refuse nothing when it comes to the girl who leans her full weight into my arm as if she needs me to hold her up. The one whose beautiful blue eyes look rather glassy right now. Is she about to get sick right here in the foyer? "Ragnhild?"

She sends me a smile every bit as fake as the one she turns on the receptionist a few seconds later as we cross the floor to the reception desk. The lady who didn't know Ragnhild as a gap-toothed six-year-old is likely fooled. Me? Not so much.

But I stand there quietly, playing the part of a *somewhat happy* fiance while Ragnhild chats away about wedding ceremonies, the weather, and more topics I tune out. After several minutes, the woman behind the desk finally gives us directions to where we can get changed. Is she always this chatty, or is she and Ragnhild friends?

Ragnhild talks a fair bit about her job, but since most of the stories tend to involve a certain Jacob, I usually try my best to tune them out. To my detriment, my brain hangs on every word she utters, including the ones about a man whose every action seems so perfect it's a wonder he's not up for sainthood. Then again, the Norwegian Seamen's Church is a protestant church, so they probably don't canonize people.

I try to remember if Ragnhild has talked about this woman. I steal a glance at the name tag stuck to her dark cardigan, but it doesn't ring any bells. None the wiser, I dip my head in a nod, and follow the girl of my dreams down a narrow, carpeted hallway. Pictures of Norwegian royals line the white walls, and a sweet, buttery aroma fills the air. Waffles? Ragnhild is always going on about waffle-duty with Jacob. I suppose the aroma could be baked into the walls.

I look down at Ragnhild just as she stops in front of a door, so abruptly I almost walk into her. My hand lands on her shoulder, and I stop my forward momentum to keep from pushing her into the door. Her red hair is like silk underneath my rough palms. I let my hand slide down her shoulder, squeezing her upper arm in a comforting gesture.

It's not what I want to do.

What I want is to push gently on that shoulder until she turns to face me. And when her surprised gaze meets mine, I want to drop the stupid garment bags still in my grip and fill my hands with her instead.

I want to kiss her until she realizes that she doesn't need to beg for the crumbs of another man's love—until she realizes that mine is given freely. Kiss her for however long it takes for her to get it into her stubborn head.

And maybe the longer the better.

I drop my hand, suddenly afraid I'll do just that—and live to rue the consequences.

"Okay, I think this is the right place." While I've been fantasizing about kissing her, Ragnhild has been studying the sign next to the door we're stopped in front of.

I want to ask if she's sure. If she's still determined to go through with this. But though she opens the door slowly with hesitation written all over the way she carefully peeks inside, her chin still has that stubborn set to it. And I know that look, and so I don't ask.

She swallows, squares her small shoulders, and walks ahead of me into the room. Her hair slips off her shoulder, calling out to my hands. I pull the door closed with my free hand to keep it occupied, shutting out the last lingering notes of the Christmas music in the reception.

I wish we were home on the farm. I wouldn't say no to a repeat of last Saturday's events. I'd much rather have her wriggling in my arms while finding every last ticklish spot under her ribs. Even if I'd be spitting out the long, red hairs finding their way into my mouth with her movements.

I smile at the memory of our tickle fight, but my smile drops as quickly as it appears. Because instead of the perfection of last Saturday, I'm hours away from home, leaning against a shelf of books in a small room filled with stuffy, buttery air. And rather than sipping my coffee, I'm waiting for Ragnhild to come out from the restroom where she's changing into her national costume to get ready for her wedding. And then it will be my turn to put on my *bunad*. And then…. I'll have to pretend to marry her.

The reality is that, barring common sense and us needing to be on the same page, I'd happily marry her for real today.

But it's not a real wedding we're preparing for. It's all an attempt to make it appear as if she's about to ride off into the sunset with me. On the off chance that a guy who hasn't found a way to ask Ragnhild out in the four months they've worked together will have an epiphany at the sight of her at the altar. It's too ridiculous to be the plot of a book, not to mention my actual life. I roll my eyes, thankful Ragnhild is the only one who knows why I'm here today. The guys at work would have a field day with this one if they knew. As would Olav.

A moment later, the bathroom door creaks, and Ragnhild emerges looking like a dream come true. Her long red hair is brushed out into a shiny mass over her shoulders, her eyes are clear and blue, and there's an uncertain smile playing on her lips. "Does it look right?"

It looks more than right. Her *bunad* fits her to a tee. Black skirts swish around her calves as she twirls in front of me, her white shirt sleeves practically billowing with the movement. Her red waist fits snugly around her chest, and silver gleams at her throat and wrists. My chest feels tight as I watch her, completely forgetting that she expects an answer.

"Is it that bad?" The hesitation is back in her voice.

"No." I cough the word out, needing her to know that immediately. "You look beautiful, and your outfit is perfect." My voice is more like a croak than anything, but it's clear that she gets the sentiment when she sends a brilliant smile my way.

Suddenly I worry that her plan *will* work. What man would take one look at this woman, and not immediately ask her out on a date? Will we even need a ceremony to turn Jacob's world upside down? Just seeing her like this, with the blush in her cheeks and the light in her eyes has to be enough. If this man is remotely interested, he'll jump at the chance.

And if he does…. Is that it for us? Will I have lost this woman forever? Without ever having told her how I feel? Will I spend the rest of my life watching Ragnhild live out her dreams with another man? Will I rock her babies on my lap and never be more than their uncle?

Or worse, what if Jacob can't handle our friendship? What if he figures out my feelings for her and tries to discourage Ragnhild from hanging out with me? What if I'm not just losing out on a chance to date the woman of my dreams today? What if this miserable Saturday is also the end of our friendship?

Suddenly, my days pining after Ragnhild while she remains blissfully unaware don't seem like such a travesty. They seem like the better end of the stick. So much better than the future I now picture.

I curl my fist around the hanger and pull the garment bag with me into the tiny bathroom. But my depressive thoughts don't let up while I change into my *bunad*. They spiral further, leaving me to feel more defeated than I have in a long time. I bend my neck to step out of the bathroom doorway.

The quick once-over Ragnhild gives me when I emerge gives me a sliver of hope. She wouldn't look at me like that if she didn't feel anything for me, would she?

I study her more closely. Her cheeks are pinker than they were before, and she doesn't quite meet my eyes as she takes my arm. We walk out of the room and down the hallway to the chapel where the ceremony is to take place. She still hasn't attempted to meet my eye, and it keeps that sliver of hope alive.

I guess it's up to Jacob now. If he has an epiphany—I've lost, and only time will tell how much. If he doesn't? Well, if he doesn't, I am done biding my time.

CHAPTER 18

RAGNHILD

"Do you, Thorleif Vaage, take Ragnhild Eilertsen to be your lawfully wedded wife?" Tingles of anticipation shimmer down my spine.

They shouldn't, but they do.

I know this isn't for real, but with Thorleif's warm palms against mine, and his full attention on me I struggle to keep my story straight. Am I wrong for the heat flooding my body? For the butterflies in my stomach—for a man I am not in love with? Maybe.

Thorleif, on the other hand, seems to have no such qualms. You'd never guess this wasn't his actual wedding day—that he's *not* professing his undying love and devotion to the woman he loves.

His voice is deep and true, and I shiver under the depth of emotion in his eyes as he promises to love and cherish me. To protect me. "Yes."

And his one word encompasses everything his eyes speak.

They're fake vows. They're fake, Ragnhild.

But with the sincerity practically emanating from the man across from me, my heart doesn't believe that. Because my brain knows that Thorleif Vaage doesn't do fake, never has. And I don't think I've really taken to heart what that means.

And now that I do, it seems a little late. Now when his hands are wrapped around mine, in front of my supervisor, my co-workers, and a random selection of strangers.

Why on earth is this my moment of truth?

My skin pebbles. Because to him, these vows are true—perhaps not in the sense that he thinks he's marrying me for real—but as far as these promises go, he means them. And he's speaking them to me.

Spellbound by the truth in his eyes and the timbre of his voice, I forget what I'm here to do. I forget why I set this in motion two weeks ago. I don't scan the room for Jacob's face, for the shock and disbelief that must be painted across it. I don't tell myself that the strong fingers wrapped around mine belong to my best friend, a man I've never even kissed.

A man I never will kiss.

The festive garlands along the sanctuary walls disappear. The brightly lit Christmas tree beside the altar is no more.

All that is here, all that is real is the soft light bathing the faint lines of Thorleif's face. The strong set of his jaw, his steady gaze on me, the tender look in his eyes; the man in front of me, vowing to stand by my side in sickness and in health. Like he always has.

The ornate silver piece pinned to his linen shirt moves as his Adam's apple bobs. Is he swallowing down emotion? For me?

His image turns watery as I blink furiously. His calloused fingers tighten around mine, and then….

Then it's my turn.

Thorleif's broad shoulders rise and fall under the black wool jacket with each steady breath as I push the sacred vows into the air of the chapel. Words repeated thousands of times but that still sound as fresh as if this moment is their first—words that cannot be cheapened even by a half-cocked plan to stage a wedding.

My best friend's eyes crinkle at the corners as I promise to obey him, and I want to laugh. I know he would if he wasn't trying to hold it in out of respect for the moment. Thorleif certainly knows I hold no skills in the area of obedience.

I close my lips over the next words, biting the inside of them and staring hard at my silver-buckled shoes until the laughter rising in my chest agrees not to escape—for now.

Fake wedding ceremony or not, falling apart with laughter during it just won't do.

My supervisor spurs me on, and I keep my eyes on the dark locks curling at Thorleif's temples as I speak. Until it feels safe to gaze into his eyes again.

Except, gazing into the dark brown depths doesn't feel safe at all. The laughter I was afraid would send me over the edge is no longer present. Another deeper emotion has taken up room in his gaze, and it makes my heart flutter deep in my chest. Watching the depth of feeling etched on his face makes my stomach roil. My head feels light and my heart lighter.

"By the power invested in me, I hereby declare you, husband and wife. *Mann og kone.*"

I glance at my supervisor for the next cue. My world feels off-kilter, falling, tilting, but surely there's more? But the man's smile is wide and proud as he looks us over, and he winks at Thorleif as he speaks the next words in Norwegian—the language that Thorleif speaks fluently, but I don't. "*Du kan nå kysse bruden.*"

My ears perk at that word in the middle. I know that word. *Kysse.* Kiss.

What? No! Reality slams into me. The glittering sanctuary bursts back into focus along with the crowd of strangers gathered, and the man who just told my best friend to kiss me.

Where are Jacob's shouted words of agony? We weren't supposed to get this far in the ceremony. Jacob was supposed to rush in when the minister asked if anyone had objections. There wasn't supposed to be kissing!

And yet, Thorleif's fingers already tighten on mine. His thumb trails across the top of my hand. His gaze searches mine as he leans in. The question in his eyes sends my stomach into somersaults. His scent is overpowering as his breath feathers my face. And I don't want this, do I?

I can't want this! Best friends are not supposed to want this.

I wet my dry lips and catch the darkening of his eyes as I do so. Because it's clear Thorleif never read that chapter of the best friends manual.

My heart thunders.

Thorleif presses his mouth to mine. His lips are soft and warm, and...gone. He pulls back, and I'm not ready for the onslaught of sensations flooding me.

Every nerve ending in my body is ablaze. My skin is too hot. My lips are flaming.

Still holding my breath, I slowly let it out, and my stomach quivers.

It wasn't even a real kiss. Why is my body freaking out? I swallow down the uncanny feeling rising in my chest. It's not disappointment tugging behind my ribs. It can't be. Not when Thorleif and I are friends and nothing more.

I don't want to kiss him. I'm not replaying the kiss.

I'm not here for that, anyways—I'm here to elicit a reaction from Jacob.

Jacob.

I stare aghast at Thorleif and turn to scan the room.

Jacob is in love with me. Or at the very least he has a big crush on me. As big as the one I've had on him. So why isn't he making a scene?

My eyes fall on the back row and the six feet of muscles and heartbreak sitting there in a blue suit. His dark eyes meet mine across the mostly empty rows. I search for a pang of grief in them, for his polite smile to fall in disappointment. But there's not a trace of hurt on Jacob's face—only a heart-stopping grin almost as wide as my supervisor's.

What is wrong with these people? I just *married* Thorleif, and Jacob doesn't even care.

In a daze, I let Thorleif lead me down the steps and the aisle. I clutch the thick black wool of his coat sleeve like the lifeline it is. I keep my smile tight as I struggle to hold my tears back through the barrage of well-wishers.

I don't hear a thing my supervisor says. Nor do I pay attention to the people fawning over my *bunad*. I can't seem to answer the questions about the embroidered stomacher behind the silver lacing, or the geographical origin of my red waist and black skirts.

Jacob slaps Thorleif's back and they exchange words I don't catch as a violent desire to disappear overcomes me. Jacob's arms wrap me in a hug.

A hug.

And my insides don't flop like they did the first time Jacob grinned at me over a burned waffle. The man whose heart was supposed to break at the very thought of losing me to another offers me nothing but a friendly hug. What a tragedy this is!

Hoping against hope that my glassy eyes pass for overwhelming joy, I bite the inside of my lip to keep from bawling. Jacob couldn't care less about keeping me all to himself. No, he's pleased to see me marry another man. All these months, I thought Jacob liked me. I thought all he needed was a nudge in the right direction—that a sharp sting of jealousy would be enough to ignite a fire in him to pursue me. I've been delusional.

And having the delusion crack so violently hurts.

My chest aches and my nose tingles as I lose the battle with my emotions, and tears blur my vision. I want to bury my head into the soft pillows of my bed at home and cry until I have no more tears.

I lean into Thorleif's warm side, wanting the giant man next to me to swallow me up. Or at least to carry me far away. "I want to go home." My voice sounds tremulous, like a child's when seconds away from a meltdown.

"I know." Thorleif's voice rumbles through his chest, against my cheek. I can't meet Thorleif's gaze; nor Jacob's; can't meet the eyes of anyone I've scammed into this ceremony.

Thorleif wraps his arm around me and leads me to the hallway we walked out of minutes before. I change out of my wedding attire and pack it up while Thorleif changes into jeans and his flannel shirt. Seeing him look so familiar in this place full of heartbreak is a balm to my soul. But then my gaze catches on his mouth, and I remember the kiss and die another small death.

We're out of the building within minutes. I close my eyes as the heavy lobby doors shut behind us, cutting off the instrumental Christmas music of the lobby for the sounds of the rumbling city in the throes of Christmas shoppers.

Chilled air closes in around us, and Christmas lights twinkle at us from every building. I keep my eyes on the broad back of the man walking down the stone steps in front of me. I don't glance behind me. In fact, once my contract ends at New Year's, I'll never darken the door of this church again.

CHAPTER 19

RAGNHILD

The subway car is as noisy and crowded on our way back as it was this morning. Except that this time, I have none of my hopes for the day to keep me from feeling choked by the massive crowd.

I don't enjoy this environment on a regular day. But today when I've had just about all my hopes crushed it's unbearable. The crowd with its loud voices and foreign smells makes bile rise in my throat, and for several long minutes, I'm worried I'll throw up right here on the subway.

I thought this day would end in triumph. I was certain that Jacob would interrupt the ceremony. Certain he'd share his true feelings with me, maybe even ask me out for a drink—but he did neither. I thought the crush I had on him was reciprocal. I thought the smiles, the secret glances, and our chemistry meant he liked me. But Jacob was more than happy to sit through my wedding ceremony watching me promise my life and love to another man.

And worse? Much worse than my misguided crush is realizing my true feelings about my best friend. Or the man who was my best friend this morning. I don't know if our friendship is still intact.

We've left the Norwegian Seamen's Church in the dust, and I'm alone with Thorleif. Well, Thorleif, the strangers in this subway car, and a massive weight of my guilt—each one pressing me relentlessly into the filthy floor.

Why did I think asking him to help me with this was a good idea? Why didn't I realize how much his friendship meant to me before I risked it as collateral damage?

I kissed Thorleif.

Or he kissed me.

But he had no choice, did he? I pulled him with me here today without taking into consideration how awkward that might be for him. But I hadn't planned on the ceremony running its course. We weren't supposed to get to the kiss.

Why didn't I realize that we might make it all the way to the kiss? Why didn't I have a plan B in place?

If he had known he'd be forced to kiss me, would he still have come? Would he still have said yes?

I groan, not so quietly I realize when I draw concerned glances from both Thorleif and two other passengers. I shake my head, hoping that will be proof enough that I'm not buckling under the weight of my terrible decisions.

Of course, he would have come with me. This is Thorleif—he would fight a coyote with his bare hands if I was in danger. Not that kissing me is exactly in that same category, but....

My stomach does another unauthorized flip as that kiss floats across my mind. It wasn't even a real kiss. He didn't touch me, only held my hands and kissed me. And still, the memory makes butter-flies come to life in my stomach.

His warm mouth touched mine. Our breaths mingled. And that tug deep within me that made me long to wrap my arms around him, slide my fingers into the hair at the back of his neck, and kiss him properly? It is still there.

I shouldn't be losing my mind over a kiss that was barely a peck. But losing my mind I am.

And I know things can't be the same between us anymore. How could they?

Even if he's still willing to be my friend, how do you go back to being only friends after kissing? How do you go back to being only friends when you're not sure only friends is something you still want?

I glance over at Thorleif and wish I could rewind the day to this morning. Wish I never deleted my text telling him I wanted to cancel this trip. Wish I pressed send instead.

We could have spent this long, sunny Saturday together at the Vaage farm. I could have curled up next to him on the couch in the living room with my book. Far from the crowds and lights and noise we'd drink coffee, sneak baked goods, and enjoy each other's company.

And maybe we wouldn't have that kiss, and I wouldn't know what his mouth feels like against mine. And there wouldn't be this hope for more unfurling inside me, but at least we'd still have a friendship to salvage.

And now? Now I don't even know if we have that.

CHAPTER 20

THORLEIF

I pay the remaining balance on the parking meter and unlock the doors to my old, green Ford. I hold the door open for Ragnhild.

"Thank you." But she doesn't even glance at me as she climbs into the cab, sliding over to the passenger side of the bench seat. We have four long hours of driving ahead of us to get back to the farm. Four more hours of watching the girl I love heartbroken because some idiot didn't have the guts to ask her out.

I don't know much about Jacob. But I do know that he's an idiot for not seeing how amazing Ragnhild is.

Two hours into the drive, all we have accomplished is a hundred and twenty minutes of stilted conversation. The sun is setting around us, and Ragnhild's hair is like orange flames in the low light. She's mere inches away, yet so out of reach. But maybe I haven't lost her completely? Maybe I still have a chance?

By the time I finally pull into the driveway, it is dark, and Saturday is more than over. We've driven the last couple of miles in the dark in complete silence.

My entire Saturday off has been spent playing dress up in the city. Not that I would have wanted to spend my day with anyone else—but I wouldn't have chosen to trail after Ragnhild between skyscrapers and crowds of Christmas shoppers, while her full focus was on another man.

She's appeared wilted ever since that look of horror right after I kissed her—if that brief meeting of lips even qualified as a kiss. It was a peck at most. But after the last few days of sizzling tension between us, I suspect it wasn't our kiss that horrified her.

Not when her confused gaze searched the rows of chairs in the chapel for the man she'd gone to all this trouble for. I didn't miss her face falling as she found him grinning—far from devastated. Could I have guessed at this outcome? Probably.

But, as intelligent as she is, I don't think Ragnhild did.

I step stiffly out of the cab—my joints feel like they belong to an old man after the long drive. Ragnhild scoots out behind me, groaning, too as she steps gingerly to the ground. I grab all our stuff from behind the seats and carry it across the driveway to the house. The *bunads* are too valuable to leave in the truck, even parked in our driveway.

The bells on the backdoor jingle as I open it and put the stuff down on the chair on the back porch. Ragnhild closes the door behind us, kicks off her boots, and walks past me to lift the blanket and enter the warm living room.

I pull off my boots and rub my arms as I duck under the blanket separating the poorly insulated porch from our living space. Bestemor is nowhere to be seen, but my mother sits in her rocking chair with her paper as usual. She folds it up and puts it on the side table next to her chair. "There's *rømmegrøt* in the fridge for both of you. I'm going to head up to bed now that you're home."

"Okay." I walk over to her and drop a kiss on her head as she stands up. My mother is not a short woman, but I am still several inches taller than her, so it's an easy feat. She peers up at me with blue eyes that see everything. Her hand comes to rest on my cheek, her voice low. "It will work out, Thorleif."

I startle because there's no way she can know where we've been, or what we've done today. But even so, her eyes cut to Ragnhild, huddling by the *Jøtul* stove. "Go comfort your girl. She looks like she's been through the wringer today."

I pull in a deep breath and let out an even deeper sigh. "She has." Apparently, I don't need to go into details. Our story must be written on our faces in a script my mother knows by heart.

She nods and pats my cheek again. "You've got this."

She's said these three words to me my entire life—about my math homework, when I fretted about asking a girl to prom, and before every job interview I've ever gone to. I don't know if I fully believe her, but I nod.

"*God natt, mor.*" Goodnight, mother.

"*God natt*, Thorleif." She smiles, then she walks over to Ragnhild, who is dejection personified. My mother wraps her strong arms around the woman I love, cradling her to her chest as if she's her daughter—and maybe she is. She whispers something in Ragnhild's ear that I don't catch, then she kisses her hair. "Goodnight, Ragnhild."

"Goodnight."

My mother turns the corner, and her footfalls are loud on the stairs. Ragnhild and I are left alone in the quiet room. The tension is thick, and I have no idea what to do to ease it.

Instead of trying, I walk into the kitchen to pull our *rømmegrøt* dinner out from the fridge. I ladle the thick porridge made from thickened sour cream into a pot, then make quick work of heating it, and the melted butterfat, up over the gas stove.

Ragnhild, finally peeling herself away from the hot *Jøtul* stove, finds bowls and cups for us. Within minutes, I drop ladlefuls of the thick, creamy porridge into the first bowl and hand it to Ragnhild.

She leans forward on the bench to take it from me, and I catch the scent of her hair as she draws close. Ragnhild's hair smells like cardamom rolls and home—like the perfect culmination of every Norwegian pastry my mother has ever pulled from the oven in this kitchen. Our fingers touch as the bowl changes hands, and a tingle runs up my arm. Her eyes meet mine for just a second before her gaze drops to the porridge in the bowl.

I turn back to the stove, but the scent of her still lingers in the air around me—heady and close. Why did I let us get so far astray? My front-row seat to all the trouble she's gone to get a reaction from Jacob has done nothing to change my mind. I want her. I want Ragnhild—with all her preposterous ideas, her impulsivity, and incorrigible optimism.

I serve up my own bowl of *rømmegrøt* and move the pot to the back of the stove. Then I turn to the girl I love—the girl who's had her heart shattered today. I pull in a deep breath, trying to obey my mother. "I know you're disappointed, and for what it's worth, I'm sorry."

I may not be sorry that her plan to ride off into the sunset with Jacob failed, but I am sorry for the sadness I sense in her dark eyes and hunched form. Ragnhild's shoulders rise and fall on a sigh. She sends me a half-smile but says nothing. How do I cheer her up? "On the bright side, there's no article accusing any of my foremothers of trying to snag the king for a husband?"

I want her to take the bait and smile fully. It's not the happiest of memories for either of us, but it does put today's disaster in a better light.

Bestemor didn't talk to me for weeks after the article aired, and my mother gave us both an earful—Ragnhild for her careless wording, and me for not stopping her. As if I hold any sort of power over the red-headed force of nature sitting at my kitchen table. The force of nature that has yet to touch her food.

I reach for the stoneware jug and pour melted butter over the porridge in both bowls, then add a sprinkle of cinnamon sugar from the wooden bowl. "Even if you *did* marry their descendant."

Ragnhild straightens a bit on the other side of the table. "The marriage license was a fake. It's not signed by the town clerk, so it's not like we're married for real. And I never *meant* to imply that any of your ancestors tried to marry into royalty by devious means."

I chuckle, still hoping I can get the sadness to slip from her eyes. "And you didn't mean for anyone to read it, either. And yet, the biggest Norwegian American newspaper in the country picked it up."

She rolls her eyes, and there's decidedly less sadness in them now. "All I wrote was that you might be related to royalty some-where back in your lineage. Saying I made accusations was a long stretch." But the conclusion had been drawn regardless, and worse, broadcasted.

Ragnhild groans and hides her face in her hands for a second. Maybe reminding her of her biggest failure wasn't what my mother had in mind when she asked me to comfort Ragnhild. I don't think I've exactly cheered her up, but the conversation seems to have distracted her at least. She straightens and picks up her spoon as if determined to succeed at something—if only at eating supper.

I follow her example, and move my first spoonful of *rømmegrøt* to my mouth. The rich, tart flavor of the meal dances on my tongue —followed by the sweet cinnamon sugar and salty butter.

My mother has made this traditional dish every Saturday for as long as I can remember. I usually heat it up on the stove when I return from work. Or, like today, when I've returned from a fake wedding ceremony in New York City. After coming very close to properly kissing the girl across the table from me. The same girl I want across the table from me for all my meals. Every day. For all the days of my life. And the only one I ever want to kiss.

We eat in silence, save for the spoons scraping against the wooden bowls, and an occasional crackle from the fire in the *Jøtul* stove in the other room. I push my chair away from the table as I go back for a refill.

Ragnhild shakes her head when I reach for her bowl to top it off, but at least she's scraped her first bowl clean by the time I finish my second. "Is Bestemor ever going to forgive me, do you think?" Ragnhild puts her spoon down, eyes so full of hope my stomach churns. But I have no say in this, no matter how much I wish I did.

"For the touring king?" Having such salacious untruths thrown in her face over coffee at the senior center had been a rough way for Bestemor to learn about the pervasiveness of the internet. "I don't know, Ragnhild. I think she knows you didn't do it on purpose, but I also think she's still hurt."

She swallows and nods, and I hate the dashed hope in her eyes. She studies the worn surface of the table intently for a minute, her jaw working. Then, without meeting my gaze, she gets up to bring her empty bowl to the sink.

I push my chair back, too, as the exhaustion of the day finally seeps in over me. I'd planned on making another cup of coffee and staying up for a bit to talk. We do need to talk. Maybe do more than talk. But I don't think I can muster the strength right now.

I stretch and yawn much deeper than planned. "Is it okay if I take you home tomorrow? I don't think I can stay awake for another hour."

"Yeah, that's fine." But Ragnhild doesn't look at all happy about the prospect of staying here until tomorrow. And I guess I don't much blame her. But we have stuff to talk about, a lot of stuff. Because once I've had some decent shut-eye; I'm going to go get the girl.

CHAPTER 21

RAGNHILD

Solsnu, December 22nd

The longest night of the year is over, and I wake to a layer of fresh snow covering the world. As if winter needs me to remember that it's here still, winter equinox or not.

As soon as I crawl out from under the covers in my shorts and tank top, chills race across my skin, and gooseflesh breaks out everywhere on my body. It would be impossible to forget that winter is here. And this particular one seems to stretch before me like an endless season of failure. Why did I think staging a wedding was a good idea?

Why couldn't I see that my friendship with Thorleif was worth a hundred relationships with a guy like Jacob? And now I might have blown it. Actually, I'm fairly certain I've completely blown it. We barely spoke on the way home yesterday, and Thorleif didn't even offer to drive me home after we'd quietly eaten our *rømmegrøt* supper.

I get dressed before I go downstairs. I don't want to run into

Thorleif in my pajamas today. I'm not entirely sure I want to run into him at all if I'm being honest. But of course, I run into him. He's always up early, even on a gray and dreary Sunday morning like this one.

"Hi." He rises from the couch when I come downstairs. His dark hair is still messy from sleep, contrasting with his blue checkered shirt and dark jeans. He's as devastatingly handsome as always. I just haven't always been ready to admit that that's what he is. Apparently, all it took was a trip to New York City and a failed fake wedding.

I wet my lips and swallow down the mortification of facing him so soon after our disastrous day yesterday. "Hi."

Thorleif holds his hand out for mine. "Come up to the field with me."

I frown, but I don't take his hand. Judging by the chill at the edges of the room, it's freezing out, and he wants to go for a stroll up to the field? "I haven't even had coffee."

He grins. "I made you a thermo cup." He nods in the direction of the coffee table where two sage green thermo cups sit waiting. He planned this?

"Did you put cream in it?"

His eyes gleam at me, but it's too early in the morning for me to interpret what that glint means. "Of course, I did. Just the way you like it."

I'm out of excuses. I yawn as I cross the room and pull back the blanket to step onto the back porch. If I thought the living room was cool, it has nothing on the back porch. My teeth chatter, and I reach for Thorleif's massive work jacket. It's the warmest one in the house.

He raises his eyebrows. "Stealing my jacket, huh?"

"You're the one forcing me outside at the crack of dawn." We're nowhere near the crack of dawn, but I'm on edge. I assume he wants to talk, and not knowing what it's about absolutely terrifies me. What if he tells me we can no longer be friends? What if this is my last morning waking up in this cozy farmhouse? The last time my bare feet touch the freezing, uneven wood floors—the last time I smell that scent of cardamom, woodsmoke, and vanilla candles lingering in the living room? My heart trembles.

Thorleif rolls his eyes and grabs his other coat. Once my coat is zipped up and I've pulled my scarf on, I reach for the thermo mug in Thorleif's hand and take my first blessed sip of coffee. It tastes like heaven. Bolstered by the warm drink, I push open the door.

The day seems brighter as we go outside. The cloud cover is lighter, and nowhere near as gray. Golden sunlight colors the wooded hill to my left as I trail behind Thorleif's hulking form up the hill. The landscape around us is covered in a soft layer of new snow. But as I step inside each of Thorleif's large boot prints on the path up to the field, gray, slushy mud clings to my boots.

The late December wind goes straight through my several layers of clothing, jeans, and wool long johns. Clearly, it doesn't know the first thing about the appropriate response to a woman raised on the sturdy Norwegian principle of there being "no such thing as bad weather, only bad clothing."

I round my shoulders and hasten my steps. I long for the leaves that shield the path from the icy winds the rest of the year. Well, in fall at least. There's a distinct lack of icy winds during the summer months—even in upstate New York.

I love all of the Vaage farm, having spent so much time here as a child—but where the path crests the hill and opens up into a wide field is the place I love the most.

Thorleif stops to hold back a snowy branch, and I duck under his arm and step into the clearing. The field is glorious—a thick blanket of white covers the expanse in front of us. Golden sunlight floats into the snowy drifts from between the trees, tipping the frosted grass at the edges of the field with sparkling light. And I understand why he wanted this conversation here.

Awed by the absolute perfection of this place, my words are barely a breath. "It's beautiful."

I sense him next to me, but I can't take my eyes off the breath-taking scene in front of me. I put my thermo cup to my mouth, sipping the hot coffee and letting it warm my insides—letting it fortify me against this conversation.

I want to be brave and face Thorleif, but how can I? I'm terrified. So I pull another sip of my coffee, eyes still on the morning sunlight dancing across the field.

"We need to talk, Ragnhild." Thorleif's voice is the one I can't argue with. The one he doesn't often use with me.

What if this is it?

My memories of Jacob end with our coffee breaks at work and the occasional late-night waffle iron duty—Thorleif is in all my memories. In my favorite ones.

How could I think the two were equal?

Thorleif is the one I sat next to on Mor Vaage's lap. I held his hand in mine as we listened in awe to her stories about her child-hood in Norway. Twenty years later, the best part of that memory is still the presence of the man standing next to me.

It doesn't matter that my hands are no longer the chubby hands of a toddler, or that he no longer sucks his thumb when he listens to Mor Vaage's stories. What if I've thrown away all of my future memories with this man? For that silly crush.

Suddenly I can't bear it anymore. I need to know that he's not breaking up with me, breaking up our friendship. I turn to him, eyes welling with tears. "I'm so sorry. I can't believe that I made you go through with that wedding. I should never have asked you."

The first tear slips over my lashes, and the next is quick to follow. "I'm so sorry, Thorleif. Please don't break up with me."

He doesn't say a word, and my eyes are too wet for me to see his expression. I finally blink my eyes enough to clear the moisture, then dare a glance at him.

Thorleif is gaping at me. "Break up what? Are we…. We're not together, are we?"

I sniff, attempting to wipe the tears from my cheeks before they freeze to my skin. But they keep coming, and it's useless. "I mean break up our friendship."

Understanding dawns in his eyes, then a look of horror. "Is that what you thought I brought you up here to do?"

"Isn't it?" I wipe my cheeks again.

"You thought I made you coffee and brought you to your favorite place to break off our friendship?" He says this as if it's the most preposterous thing he's heard in his life. But as much time as he spends with me, it can't possibly be.

I nod, and he stares incredulously at me for another minute. Then he laughs—a deep, rich sound that fills the field with warmth, and my heart with hope. He shakes his head. "That is not at all what I asked you up here for. God, I can't believe you'd think that of me."

I frown, not understanding why he is laughing. "Why wouldn't I? I've treated you horribly. I don't deserve to be your friend."

He swallows, suddenly serious. "Well, I don't exactly want you to be that."

I close my eyes as pain holds my heart in a vise. He doesn't want to be friends. I'm ready to turn tail and run. I cannot face a future where Thorleif and I aren't friends. I absolutely can not. I'll walk home if I have to.

But then he continues speaking, and I open my eyes again. "Because I'd like us to be more than that." His gaze meets mine, so steady, so hopeful, my pulse speeds up. My heart thunders in my chest.

He speaks slowly, hesitantly, as his gaze searches my face for any clues. "Is that something…you'd like, too?"

I can't speak. All my words are frozen on my tongue as I try to wrap my brain around the ones that just escaped his lips. Thorleif wants to be more than friends.

I shouldn't be so shocked. This isn't news to me. I've suspected it this whole month, and more so in the last two weeks. I know we have chemistry in buckets, that we know each other about as well as you can know someone. I know that I've spent weeks distracting myself from admitting that I want to kiss him. But is that enough?

I pull in a deep breath.

His gaze measures me from head to toe, lingering on my eyes. "If you don't, I swear I'll back off, Ragnhild. For real this time." But his words sound hollow—as if this option doesn't excite him at all, and the sadness in his eyes tears at my heartstrings.

I swallow, trying to find enough moisture for my tongue to speak the words that will push away that sadness before it lingers. "I don't want you to back off."

Thorleif's entire body stills. He turns to me with the most intense gaze I've ever received from anyone. No less him. "Did you just…. You don't?"

I shake my head. "I don't want you to back off. But I also need you to know that I'm absolutely terrified, and I don't know how to do any of this, and—"

Thorleif's hand wraps around mine, tugging me close to him, and cutting my verbal freak-out session short. "I don't need you to know how to do any of this." His words are low and soothing. A smile slips into his voice. "Although I suspect you already know how."

I hold my breath as we stand surrounded by the frozen winter morning. My cheeks are still damp with my earlier tears, and I'm shivering. Thorleif wraps his arms around me and pulls me flush against his body. "You're cold."

I nod, just barely able to keep the chatter of my teeth from cutting off my words. "I'm very cold."

His eyes shine down at me, and I hold my breath. He stills, glancing at the arm he's wrapped around my shoulder. "This is alright, right?" Concern slips into his voice, and I simultaneously hate that he's so unsure of himself and love that he's checking in with me.

"This is fine." I know he's holding me very close, but there are so many layers of clothes between us that it doesn't feel quite as intimate as it probably is. Thorleif hesitates, then lowers his head to brush a kiss against my cold cheekbone. One more kiss under my eye, and my eyes flutter closed as he continues to kiss the tears from my cheeks.

When he stops, I open my eyes.

He's grinning down at me. "I've wanted to do that for a very long time." He kisses my nose, and I melt like a snowflake in morning sunlight.

He doesn't hate me for making him stage a wedding. He doesn't want to break up with me. And…he wants to be more than friends.

Maybe this won't be so bad?

CHAPTER 22

RAGNHILD

Christmas is two days away, and to say that I'm scrambling to get ready is an understatement. It's not like I have my own household and need to worry about cooking for a mass of people or anything like that. I don't even have children who need presents and magic. But I've always got big plans for homemade gifts that I start way too late, and then I spend the last few days before the holidays frantically catching up. This year is no different.

Except, that I haven't seen as much of Thorleif as I'm used to. Not since this morning when our walk in the field was cut short when Mor Vaage needed his help with something or other at the house. I know he's been busy with last-minute cleaning, wiping cobwebs off of the beams upstairs, and the like, so I'm sure he isn't avoiding me. But what if he is?

I'm tucked away upstairs in my room, where my last-minute Christmas present preparations are least likely to be discovered. I wrap a satin ribbon around the jar of white and red striped peppermint candies. *Polkagriser*, Bestemor calls them. They're her favorite candy, and it took me quite a bit of online research to track these down.

I pull the ends of the bow until it's just right before I'm

distracted by thoughts of Thorleif and me again. What if our morning in the field wasn't enough to clear the air between us? He was pretty clear about what he wanted, but was I?

"Hey, you." Thorleif's voice breaks off my train of thought, sending my pulse into an erratic skitter. I turn to find him right behind me, standing in my doorway—eyes dark and hopeful. "Were you planning on going home, or do you have time to go for a walk with me?"

My entire body tingles at his nearness, his at-least-three-feet-away-ness. Just sharing this space with him feels strangely intimate. Is *walking* code for something now that we're more than just friends? I want to ask him, but I don't want to sound stupid, so I just nod.

"Good. I feel like I haven't seen you all day." He grins, and my heart jumps into my throat. How have I managed to keep an even blood pressure around this man for so many years?

I put down the jar of candies before it slips out of my trembling hand.

Closing the door behind me, I follow him downstairs. Soon, the cold night surrounds us as we walk up to the field. It looks different from what it did this morning. I tilt my head back until I can see the thousands of stars crowding the dark skies above us.

I've always been scared of the dark, but never when I'm with Thorleif. Sensing his steady presence behind me, I close my eyes and marvel at the absence of the clawing fear in my chest. I doubt Jacob could ever have made me feel like this.

My fingers fumble for Thorleif's. A content sigh escapes my lips as I find them, and his large, warm hand wraps around mine. "This field is so quiet."

Thorleif rubs his thumb across my hand, sending delicious sparks up my arm. He doesn't comment on my words, but I've long since learned to field my own conversations. And this is a conversation I need to have with him. "It feels like heaven compared to the city yesterday, doesn't it?"

He grunts, and I tuck closer to him and tilt my head to meet his eyes. "Which do you like better?"

He looks down at me, sending my stomach into a somersault. The timbre of his voice resonates through my bones as if his voice has infiltrated the air. "You have to ask me that?"

Another shiver trickles down my spine, not from the cold, but from the heat in his eyes. No, I don't need to ask this homegrown country boy which he prefers. He told me once that no city lights could ever hold a candle to a starry sky over the field we're standing in right now. His smile is a flash of white teeth in his beard. "Also, your color is better here, and I don't think you're about to pass out."

I roll my eyes, even though I feel nowhere near as steady on my feet as usual. I smile back up at him, knowing I don't need to reply. This man has been at my side in all my years of instigating trouble— he already knows he's right. I sigh. "I don't know what I was thinking, dragging you away to the city like that."

"Oh, the city was okay." A smile lurks in his voice. "I came. I saw. I kissed a girl. *Veni, vidi, vici.*" The rough pad of his finger runs down my cheek, and his touch sets off fireworks under my skin.

"I came, I saw, I conquered." My skin heats at the thought of that kiss, more so when considering the ridiculous plan I concocted.

Thorleif grins, his fingertip lingering at the corner of my lips. "I like this color on you, too." His voice warms me down to my toes, and I close my eyes, relishing his touch.

"Do you?" I breathe the question against the finger now resting on my bottom lip. Then it traces my chin, my jaw, my ear.

"About that kiss?" Thorleif hesitates, his hand pausing again. My eyes flutter open, but there's no hesitation in his eyes. "It wasn't a very good one, was it?"

"Is it even a real kiss when done under duress?" I shake my head and laugh, but my skin tingles with nerves. I'm fairly certain I know where this conversation is leading, and I'm equal parts excited and terrified.

Thorleif scoffs. "Duress? Yeah right. As if kissing you could ever be any such thing." My face flames. Is it really Thorleif saying these things to me? My Thorleif?

My heartbeat quickens because it is—and his words are a balm on my heart.

The night draws tighter around us, cocooning us into a world where it's just the two of us. Thorleif tugs on my hand wrapped around his, bringing me closer. My stomach jolts as I face him. When did he get so tall that I have to tilt my head back this far to meet his eyes?

I only know that *when* I do his dark eyes are full of wonder, of calm, of love. Full of unspoken promises I hope he'll speak one day soon. Thorleif frames my cheek with his free hand, and the seconds that pass before he touches his lips to mine feel like a lifetime.

Maybe two lifetimes.

And then my mind goes blank.

His mouth is warm and solid, and the whole world tilts around us. Stars burst behind my eyes, and starlight seeps into my veins. Because this? This is definitely a kiss. I brace my hand against his shoulder, and his strong fingers slide into my hair. Tilting the back of my head, he angles deeper, and oh, my, word—I think I might faint!

"Ragnhild, you have no...." His voice is breathy and hoarse as it trails off into another hot press of his lips to mine.

My stomach flips as I move my hands to the prickly scruff on his neck. I shove my fingers into his thick hair, tugging the strands between my fingers until he groans into my mouth. The sound does weird things to my insides.

"You have no idea how long...." He slides his hands down my back, pressing me ever closer to him, and I don't want to be anywhere else but here—with no one else but him.

Thorleif pulls away long before I'm ready, his breathing as ragged as mine. "That was a better one, huh?" His murmur against my temple triggers an uneven laugh as I struggle to recover the breaths he's stolen. The cold winter air doesn't help at all.

"Yeah. That was a kiss."

Thorleif presses one more kiss to my temple, and I want to sink into the perfection of him—of this.

"Next time I'm thinking we should get a valid license." It's the last thing I expect him to say, and my breath falls out in a rush. It's a ludicrous idea, and yet, only happiness fills my chest at the thought of marrying him for real. Does he really want to marry me?

I rest my cheek against his chest. "We already had a ceremony. Don't we just need to file our license with the town clerk?"

His laughter rumbles against my ear as his strong arms tighten around me. His breath warms my hair as he kisses the top of my head. "Yeah, that's not forward at all, Ragnhild."

I giggle into his neck. "Who'd ever accuse me of being forward? It's not like I'd ever think of dragging my best friend to fake a wedding in front of my work crush."

Thorleif pulls away enough for our eyes to meet. The intense emotion in his gaze matches his serious voice. "Is that all he was to you? A work crush?"

I slide my hands out of his and frame his face with my palms. His beard is soft against my wrists as my fingertips hover over the curls by his temples. "I never felt for him like I do for you. You know I fall in love easily—"

He snorts. "Do I ever." And I feel a stab of guilt for all the times I've made him my therapist following the breakups of my short-lived relationships.

"But those feelings aren't deep, not abiding." I hesitate, not sure if I'm ready to share what I think I've felt for a while now. "I've never loved any of them like I love you."

My words spill into the winter night, freezing any movement around us. Thorleif goes as still as a statue. The wind crackling through the brush quiets, too. The field is eerily quiet—as if Thorleif and all the world are collectively holding their breaths. "You love me?"

Tears well in my eyes at the uncertainty in his voice. How was I so consumed by my crush on Jacob that it blinded me to the very real feelings I have for this man? The man who has, and always will, love me better than a thousand Jacobs? My best friend who has watched me make a fool of myself more times than I can count and still has no misgivings about my sanity?

I gaze into the dark brown depths of his eyes and see the reflection of emotions I've denied for so long. Much too long not to speak them now.

I wet my lips, close my eyes, and swallow one last time before I hold his gaze. "I love you, Thorleif Vaage, so much."

CHAPTER 23

THORLEIF

December 23rd, Lille Julaften (little Christmas Eve)

The scent of fresh balsam fir hits my nostrils as I push open the creaking door to the backroom. The laughter and conversation from the kitchen fades as I slide it closed, and the chill of the room seeps through my shirt sleeves as soon as the latch clicks behind me.

I put the tree in the stand earlier, with Bestemor watching to make sure it was straight. Once my mother and grandmother's job, it's now mine. While many Americans decorate their trees the day after Thanksgiving, my mother holds her Christmas traditions from her childhood in Norway with a steel grip. And that includes decorating the tree on the evening of the twenty-third of December—and not a moment before.

Growing up, I never got to see it until the next morning, on *Julaften*, Christmas Eve. But I'm no longer the bleary-eyed little kid tiptoeing down the stairs while night still lingers, hand in hand with the neighbor's little girl to see the finished tree. It's been years since

I've crawled behind the couch to plug in the lights only to peek over the back of it to watch the sparkle of tinsel and lights reflect in the round, upturned face of my best friend.

Back then, Ragnhild used to cry herself to sleep on Christmas Eve, so her awed expression on those mornings made my small chest puff out with pride. I was never allowed to stay up late to help decorate then, but I *had* been the one to turn on the lights. The one who'd made those teary, grief-stricken eyes shine with joy.

Will she watch them with me this year? Maybe Ragnhild hasn't outgrown that tradition like she has her halo of red curls?

The door shuts quietly behind me, and soft footsteps move across the creaky floor. Does she think she can sneak up on me that easily?

She's next to me in a heartbeat, but she doesn't say anything. I'm about to turn around when a small, icy hand slips under my shirt. The chill burns my warm skin, and I gasp. "What in the...."

The peals of Ragnhild's laughter fill the air about me, her breath warming my neck as I twist away from her. That little witch tries to slip her frozen hand under my shirt again, but I grab it before she has a chance to.

She yelps, and I immediately loosen my hold. "You okay?"

But Ragnhild only takes advantage of my concern, snatches her hand out of my grip, and presses her cold fingers against my neck.

I growl. Does she have any idea how insanely cold her fingers are? Can she even feel them? More of her sweet laughter sounds in my ear while she twists and turns her soft body in my arms, struggling to get away.

As if I'll let that happen a second time.

I tighten my arms around her until she can no longer wriggle.

"Where the hell did you keep that hand?" I shudder, still feeling the imprint of her freezing skin on my neck. "I've probably got frostbite."

She laughs and spits out a mouthful of orange hair gone rogue during her escape attempt, but pure mischief glints in her blue eyes. "The chest freezer."

I shake my head, pushing down the laughter rising in my chest, and narrow my eyes at her. "Only you. No sane person would stick their hand into a chest freezer only to pull off a prank like this."

She snorts and rolls her eyes. "Don't flatter yourself. I was pulling out the pork ribs for dinner tomorrow. I had to dig for it."

"And you thought it was the perfect opportunity to give me frostbite?"

"Absolutely." She tugs at the arm I've got firmly in my grip. "Can I have my hand back now?" I shake my head. Never.

In fact, I'd like to ask formally for that hand soon. I push down the smile that threatens to spill onto my face and shoot her a stern look instead. "Did you come to help me decorate the tree?"

She swallows and stops her attempts to get away. Her big blue eyes are locked on my face, her gaze like a caress as it drops to my lips, then rises to mine again. "Is that what you're doing back here?"

My pulse speeds up, and hope sparks in my chest. "Did you come for anything else?" I don't care that my voice has dropped an octave. *Please please, tell me you came for something else. Like a kiss. Like you wanted to be alone with me.*

I loosen my iron grip on her shoulder and let my other hand trail down to slip around her waist. My fingers are itching to slide underneath the hem of the knit sweater she's wearing, but I hold them back. It's not yet time for that.

While my feelings for her are old, this relationship is still brand new. It's been less than twenty-four hours since our walk to the field, and I want to give her time to get comfortable with this—with me. Well, the me who wants to kiss her, and doesn't much feel like keeping my hands off her.

But I also feel the ache of every one of those twenty-four hours that have passed since I kissed her last. Has she been keeping her distance on purpose? Or has she been busy with last-minute

Christmas preparations? Surely she can't have that much to prepare?

Ragnhild's fingers curl around mine, sending shudders of want over my skin. Her free hand rests on my bicep, and there's not a hint of hesitation in her movements. The tension in my shoulders eases. It must not have been on purpose, then.

In the past Ragnhild has usually stayed over at our house the night before Christmas Eve, so she can spend all of the Christmas week, *romjula*, with my family. It's been that way since her mother left her with us over Christmas the first winter they lived here. Has she changed her mind about sleeping over in light of everything that happened yesterday? I swallow, trying not to let my nerves, or my eagerness, slip into my voice. "You're still staying here tonight?"

She nods, but pink spreads across her cheekbones as she meets my gaze. "Not in your room, though." Her gaze drops to the floor between our feet, and she flushes even deeper. God, she's so cute—I can't stand it.

I grin like a fool, and I'm pretty sure having her around is going to make me that. "I wasn't expecting you to stay in my room." But I would have said yes if she'd asked, probably quite prematurely. I don't think we're ready for that step, as much as we might want it.

The furious blush in her cheeks makes me want to kiss her again.

No, that's a lie.

I've wanted to kiss her the whole time—the blush has nothing to do with it.

Wanting to tip her chin up with my finger, but also not wanting to let go of her to do so, I wait until she lifts her face to mine. It seems to take half a lifetime, but then…finally. Her eyes are so blue, so wide, and I worry that the hesitation I see there isn't because this is new at all.

"Ragnhild?"

She holds my gaze but doesn't answer. But she doesn't have to. I read so much in that gaze, probably more than she realizes is there —insecurity, disappointment, hope.

Jacob had his chance, and he missed it. I'm not going to do the same. Not with this beautiful woman in front of me—the one who is my best friend, maybe my girlfriend. And who hopefully, one day very soon will be even more than that.

I clear my throat, but it doesn't change the husky tone of my voice. "You are worth so much more than a second glance, and you don't ever need to stage a wedding to prove it. Any man who can't see what's before his eyes without your effort isn't worth your time."

Tears glisten in Ragnhild's eyes, and she presses her lips together. "Really?"

I want to throttle Jacob for the wavering uncertainty in her voice. I want to track down her mother and give her a piece of my mind for barely checking in on her daughter all these years—for leaving this girl to think she needs to move mountains to deserve love. But I can't hunt either of them down right now, and neither are they the most important. The girl in my arms is. "Really."

A tear spills over her pale lashes and tracks down her cheeks, and I dip my head and kiss it off her hot skin. Her grief is wet and salty on my tongue. I kiss another tear, then her nose. Then I move to her mouth—a mouth that is as hungry as mine. *And, thank God, there is no hesitation there.*

I think I black out for a moment from sheer bliss—and then, when I'm back, I kiss her again. Long and deep. A forever kind of kiss.

I come up for air and press my lips to the smile that flickers at the corner of hers. Once. Twice. Catch her laughter with a third. She pulls away, but with my arm tight around her, she can't go far. And that's exactly how I want it.

"Don't we need to get to decorating that tree?" Her voice is short of breath and full of things that make me think she's not ready to trade me, or my kisses, for a collection of dusty ornaments just yet. I know I'm not.

"I don't know. Do we? I think the ornaments will keep." I kiss her nose, and she laughs again.

"Thorleif!" But my name is soft on her lips, breathless as she tugs the strands of hair at my neck. Fireworks of happiness, rise, whine, and explode inside me—mirroring the emotion in her eyes. Another kiss, and more of that laughter of hers that makes my chest light.

And I've changed my mind. She's definitely staying with me tonight.

CHAPTER 24

RAGNHILD

They say all good things must come to an end. And our make-out session next to the still undecorated tree comes to an end rather quickly when the backroom door creaks open behind us.

I jump away from Thorleif, but his arms aren't quite as quick to drop, and Mor Vaage's eyes are dancing with mirth when they meet mine. "I just wanted to say that the last box of decorations is on the table in here. Thorleif, you can come out here and bring it in." She grins, those blue eyes still sparkling with knowing. "If your hands are free."

Thorleif makes a sound I can't interpret, and his skin seems a shade darker than it should be in the half-light. But he makes no rebuttal to her comment as he trudges past her.

Mor Vaage's gaze follows him fondly as he walks through the door. Then her kind, knowing eyes meet mine, making me think she knows even the parts she didn't glimpse just now. "All is well then?"

I nod, even though my cheeks burn with embarrassment. "Yes."

Because it is. It really, really is.

This woman has known me since I was a preschooler, and I've seldom been quite as well as I am now.

"Good. I'm glad you two worked it out." And I can tell she means it. I have no idea what it's like to watch your son fall in love, but from the quiet contentment on Mor Vaage's face, I imagine it's a good feeling. And from all the friends to lovers romances that have somehow found themselves into my secret romance stash, I think it's a fair guess that she's not unhappy with where his affections have landed.

"Thank you." I bite my lip. "For letting me stay here all these years."

Another smile spreads across her face like a sunrise, starting at her lips and shining full and warm in her eyes. "You're more than welcome, Ragnhild. I wish you could have a home with your mother, but when she couldn't give you that, I'm happy we could." She hesitates. "And even if things don't work out between Thorleif and you, you'll always be welcome here. You'll always be my daughter."

And I can't say anything to that. Because my eyes burn and my throat is too tight, too unwilling to let any noise slip past it. I nod instead and press my lips tight. And she does, too, as if we share this overwhelming emotion.

When Thorleif pushes through the door, his brows lower over his dark eyes as he frowns—first at me, then at his mother. "You made her cry?"

I sniff, and laugh a teary laugh. "Thorleif. You're giving massive 'hurt her and you'll die' vibes...directed at the wrong person."

He frowns at me as if he doesn't quite know what I mean by that. But his mother does, and she laughs, full and deep, while Thorleif continues towards me and the tree.

He shifts the box of decorations to his other arm and swipes a tear away from my cheek with his free hand. "Are you okay?"

"Very." I sniff and smile up at him, and the way my joy echoes in the depths of his eyes, I'm very certain that he'd kiss me again if his mother wasn't standing right there watching us. As soon as the door shuts behind her, he does.

A long, deep kiss that makes my toes curl.

Frank Sinatra starts crooning from the other room, and I grin against Thorleif's mouth. "Do you think she's trying to tune us out? That's quite the change from the Alf Prøysen folk tunes she usually plays."

He snorts, but there's laughter in his eyes as he smirks down at me. "I don't think we're being that loud. And Frank Sinatra was in the mafia, so I don't know exactly what message she's trying to send by playing his music."

I gasp. "He was what? Are you pulling my leg?"

He sets down the box so he can wrap both arms around me. Then he presses a kiss to my nose, and I melt just a little further into him. "You didn't know that?"

"No, I didn't know that! How was I supposed to know that?"

He shrugs, one hand absentmindedly stroking up and down my back. "I guess it's common knowledge."

I tighten my hands around his waist. "Not common enough that I'd heard of it!" Which doesn't say a whole lot, even if I have been a major Sinatra fan since I was in high school.

Thorleif drops his arms from around me, and I immediately miss them. I suppose it's not possible to decorate a tree while wrapped around another person, though, so I bear my disappointment valiantly. Thorleif pulls one of the cardboard boxes closer. It screeches across the wood floor. "What do we do first? Lights?"

I roll my eyes. As if he doesn't know that after being in charge of the decorating since he was twelve. "Yes, lights first." But I can't help but tease him just a tad. What else would be the purpose of dating your best friend? "Did all that kissing scramble your brain?"

He shifts his gaze to mine—dark and heated, and full of mischief —but he doesn't move away from the box. "Maybe a little." He smirks, and I feel the effects of that smirk all the way to my toes. "We might have to unscramble it again in a little bit."

He turns back to the box he's still bent over and pulls the flap open, but only tiny red knit hats and paper angels stare back at us. No lights in that box.

I lean over to tug on another box. "This one marked 'lights,' maybe?" I raise my eyebrows as I look up at him.

He narrows his eyes. "Smart ass."

But then he grins and moves close enough to give me a smack.

I let out a gasp and jump out of his way. "Thorleif! That is not proper behavior while decorating the Christmas tree! And while even the mafia choir is urging us to bring peace on earth?"

He grins and shrugs. "I feel peaceful with my decision." His eyes dance, but I ignore them and make sure to move to the other side of the box before I bend over again to retrieve the bundled lights.

That maneuver is not lost on Thorleif. "You're alright with that, right?" There's no teasing in his voice now, only concern that he might have crossed a boundary we haven't yet discussed.

My heart warms at the honest worry in his gaze, and I wipe the smirk off my face. "Yes." Because I'm very okay with it. Which surprises me, because Thorleif and I have dated for what, forty-eight hours? My other relationships have moved a lot more slowly than this one, but none of my other boyfriends have been this concerned about getting my consent.

Boyfriend. My stomach thrills at that thought. Is that what he is, my boyfriend?

His eyes light, and the tension on his brow fades. "Good."

But when I lift the lights out of the box, and he reaches out for me again, I pull away and speak in my sternest voice. "Not in front of the Christmas lights! You can't corrupt them like this!"

He startles and drops his hands immediately. Then he laughs and helps me to unwind them. But each time our fingers brush, a jolt of electricity speeds up my arm. How is the air around us so charged? How in the world have I managed to be so close to him for so long and never felt any of this before? Were these reactions latent under my skin all this time?

I plug the extension cord in behind the couch and hand the first part of the shining lights to Thorleif. "Here, I don't want to try to reach the top."

He takes them, the bundle of lights like splatters of sunshine in his hands. His brows rise. "What do you mean you don't want to?"

I shake my head. "I mean, you're taller, so it makes sense that you'd wrap it around the top part. Why else do Norwegian men grow so tall if it's not to put the Christmas lights on for their women?"

His brows stay up, although a gleam of light enters his eyes at those last two words. "You're not that short."

He's not wrong, of course. I'm five feet seven, and three-quarters, which is more than tall enough to reach the top of the balsam fir. But I'll have to stretch to do so, and with the mood Thorleif is currently in, I suspect he's more likely to tickle me than leave me alone. And I won't be exposing my ribs to attack like that if I don't have to. "You're still taller. Work smarter, not harder, remember? This is me working smarter by having you do the work for me."

He stares at me, but I see the twitching of a smile on his lips. "Is that what it is?"

He stalks towards me, and my stomach drops—deliciously so. "Yeah, that's what it is." But my voice is barely a breath.

And when he's next to me, wrapping those big strong arms around me, I'm suddenly unwell in the best way. He turns towards him, and part of the light string drops down, wrapping around my knees as my body turns. "Not you trying to sneak out of the work?"

I shake my head emphatically. "No, I would never do that. Not with the mafia present."

But the only known mafia member in the vicinity is currently questioning whether reindeer know how to fly from the other room, and it doesn't feel like much of a threat.

"No?" Thorleif's voice is deep and full, and it ricochets through my bones. I step up onto his sock-clad feet, stretching so we're just about face to face. And I'm proving myself a liar because this man is at least as tall as the Christmas tree next to us. His fistful of Christmas lights press against my lower back, pushing me closer to his warm, solid body.

"Out of the question." I speak the words into his bearded jaw, then press a kiss to his neck. His sharp intake of breath tells me everything I need to know.

The Christmas lights drop to the floor behind me, and both of his hands frame my face. "I don't believe you."

But I have no retort to that because his mouth is on mine. And neither mafia members nor the undecorated Christmas tree can convince me to stop the absolute magic twirling to life between us. It's all I can do not to topple off of my perch. But then he hoists me higher—and with my legs wrapped around him, I'm not in danger of falling anymore.

But…I have other concerns.

"Thorleif! Not in front of the Christmas lights!"

But he doesn't listen.

Not at all. And…it's not like I want him to.

CHAPTER 25

THORLEIF

Both my mother and Bestemor have long since retired by the time we finish decorating the tree. I've turned down the lights, and have had my last cup of coffee in front of the *Jøtul* stove.

It's been a long day. A long week. But Ragnhild is showing no signs of being ready for sleep. When I walk into the kitchen to rinse out my coffee mug, she's in the process of sneaking another fresh *sirupssnipp* from under the kitchen towel. She bites into the chewy diamond-shaped cookie, making it to the halved almond in the middle before I'm done with my eye roll.

"Did you need anything?" She raises innocent eyebrows at me, but her blue eyes sparkle.

"Yeah, I figured since you've already ventured down the path of debauchery"—I nod my head towards the stolen cookie in her hand—"you might just want to keep going and stay over in my room tonight."

Ragnhild chokes on her next bite. Coughing and sputtering until her face is redder than Rudolph's nose. I'm torn between laughter and offering first aid. "Are you okay?"

She coughs again. "Not nearly."

I step closer to pat her back, but she slides away, hissing at me like a wild animal. "Not helping."

When she's dried her tears and somewhat regained her composure, she turns to me. "I can't believe you'd compare my quality testing of Christmas cookies to debauchery!"

"Is that a yes?"

She bites her lip. "To staying in your room?"

I hold her gaze. "I'm not expecting anything to happen. I just want to hold you—like that night we fell asleep on the couch. Nothing more than that." I frown. "Except my bed is significantly more comfortable. And my down comforter is much longer than that silly little wool throw."

Her cheeks go pink when I mention that night on the couch. Maybe that memory isn't quite as innocent as it sounds. But even though she's still frowning, the wrinkle between her brows seems to have smoothed a little. "And we'd be wearing what?"

I frown. "Pajamas? I'm not expecting you to show up naked." I speak without thinking, but I don't regret my words when she turns so red I swear she could heat this house on her own—without help from the *Jøtul* stove. I can't help but tease her. "Not that I'd complain, mind you."

It's true that I wouldn't complain, but I don't think it would be a smart decision either. Not when our relationship is so new and she's so recently come around to it. Truth be told, I know I'm pulling it a bit too far just by joking around with her like this.

I push the laughter from my voice. "Seriously, Ragnhild. I just want to hold you. Think of it as a sleepover." She nods, but I'm a little worried she'll change her mind. Am I asking too much of her too soon?

"I'm going up to change." She doesn't stop to hug me goodnight, but why would she if I'll see her in a little bit? I hope that's the reason she doesn't.

I turn the light off in the kitchen and slowly ascend the steps to my room. I change into my pajamas and slip under the covers. This room is much too cold for me to just stand here waiting out in the open.

My door creaks open not even five minutes later, and Ragnhild slips inside. Her long legs shine white in the half-light, and I realize I've made a severe miscalculation. "Ragnhild, what the hell are you wearing?"

She pauses, eyes wide. "Pajamas?" She phrases it like a question, which it most definitely is. I'm wearing respectable winter pajamas —flannel pajama bottoms and a T-shirt. Ragnhild is wearing a tank top and shorts that cut off at the top of her thighs.

"In the middle of winter, those are the pajamas you wear?" I swallow. I don't know how I'll be able to hold her all night, and remain sane till morning—not with all that skin inches away.

She frowns. "My room is right over the wood stove downstairs, it gets warm at night."

Keeping warm isn't an issue we'll have in this room—I'm quite certain the temperature is up by several degrees already. "I didn't know you were going to wear that."

She bites her lip. "Do you not want me to stay?"

I shake my head, and she drops her gaze to her feet and makes a soft sound that tears at my heart. I spring from the bed before I can think better of it. "No. No, that's not what I meant at all. I want you here." A little too much for my own good.

I step close to her and hold my arms out. She slips into them as easily as if we do this every night, but her eyes are worried when she gazes up at me. "Are you sure? I don't know why you asked me to do this. I'm not sure it's a good idea."

I press a warm kiss to her lips, and the worried lines on her forehead fade a bit. One more kiss, a tug on her bottom lip, and her eyes flash with something a lot closer to happiness. She tucks her cheek close to my chest, and I tug her just a tad bit closer. "I just wanted to hold you, and I couldn't quite wait until tomorrow to see you again."

I feel her lips pull into a smile against my T-shirt-clad chest, and she sighs. "That's actually pretty sweet."

I rest my chin on the top of her hair, loving the feel of her against me. Loving everything that's currently happening between us. "Yeah, I got the idea from *Falling in Love With My Best Friend.*"

She gasps. "What?"

I grin into her hair, loving that I finally get to tell her this secret, too. "It's at the top of your secret stash of romance novels."

She sucks in a breath. "You know about my romance novels?" Her cheekbones darken in the dim light from the window. Is she blushing?

God, I want to kiss her again. But I want to make her squirm a little more first. "I know about that secret, yeah. And I planted that book more than a week ago."

She pulls far enough away that she can see my face, and gapes at me. "You did not!"

I laugh. "I absolutely did."

"I thought it was Mor Vaage or Bestemor trying to put ideas in my head." She gasps, and her eyes go wide. "Did you plant the Viking chief one, too? That one was pretty spicy." She pulls the word spicy out, each syllable lasting several seconds.

"What?" My throat feels raw as the word grates across it. I've only ever planted best-friends-to-lovers books. "I definitely did not plant a spicy Viking book in your stash."

She frowns. "Whoa. I guess that must have been Mor Vaage or Bestemor, then. See, I thought the worst part was when he—"

I close my hand over her mouth, cutting her off. "I do not want to know anything about what kind of romance novels my mother or Bestemor read. Please don't ever tell me what's in that book." She nods vigorously, blue eyes so earnest I loosen my fingers just a tad.

"But they do some *crazy*—"

My hand muffles her words again. "I said no."

Mischief sparkles in her eyes, daring me to drop my hand again. Does she think she's the only one who can play dirty? I slip my other hand around her waist, pulling her even tighter against the front of my body.

Her eyes widen, and I tilt my head until only my hand separates our mouths. I kiss her cheek. Her nose. The corner of her jaw. "If I drop my hand, are you going to tell me what was in that ungodly book, or are you going to kiss me?" She nods.

I hesitate, not quite trusting the innocence in her eyes. "You mean that you'll kiss me, right?"

Bright laughter shines in her eyes, overpowering the innocence there with pure mischief. She shakes her head, and I groan.

I'm never going to be able to drop this hand.

I'm going to have to go through life with one hand plastered against her mouth. It's going to make my daily routine extremely complicated, but there's no way I can let go. No way I'm going to be able to come back from knowing what was in that book.

I'm still holding Ragnhild pressed up against me, but I'm starting to seriously miss my warm bed. The wood floor is freezing under my feet, and the cold slowly finds every bare piece of skin on my body.

Will I be able to hoist her up into my arms without letting go of her mouth? I can do this for the rest of the night as long as we're under the covers.

I slide my free arm down to her thighs—her very bare thighs.

Maybe this wasn't such a great idea.

But I've gotten this far, and this is no time to retreat. In another second I have her in my arms. Ragnhild's squeal is muffled under my palm.

I lower my brows in a mock scowl. "Shh! Don't wake up the rest of the house."

"Move your hand." Her words are hot and garbled against my fingers.

I search her eyes as if I have any way of anticipating her next move. "And you'll keep your mouth shut about Viking romance rituals?"

Her eyes dance with mischief as she grins, and I feel her flash of teeth against the back of my fingers. "I wouldn't call them romantic, but yes." I drop my hand from her mouth, but mostly because I'll drop her if I don't.

I carry her over to my bed and put her down in the spot where the comforter is still pulled back from when she came in here. I move one foot off the wood floor and onto my other foot. "Scoot over. It's freezing out here."

She rolls her eyes, but she does move over and let me slide in next to her. The blessed warmth of the comforter wraps around me, separating my skin from the cool air in my bedroom. I shift, and my foot rubs up against a bare calf. Ragnhild's calf.

I cannot believe that Ragnhild is in my bed.

What are the chances that I fell on the ice and knocked my head earlier today? Is this some sort of fever dream? She moves closer to me, legs tangling with mine, and there's no way this could be a dream. It's too good. Too solid.

"I made it up, you know." She mumbles the words into my shoulder.

I frown, trying to keep my focus on her words, and not her warm breath against my collarbone. "Made up what?"

"The spicy Viking book. There's nothing like that in that pile."

I groan. Ragnhild *would* make something like that up. "Thanks for the several minutes of internal torture."

"You're welcome." She snuggles even closer to me, her hair ending up in my mouth as usual. But I don't care—if a mouthful of hair is the price for sleeping with her in my arms, I'll gladly pay it. "Good night, Thorleif."

I wipe the hair out of my mouth and wrap an arm around her so her head rests on my shoulder. "Good night."

CHAPTER 26

THORLEIF

December 24th, Julaften morgen (Christmas Eve morning)

It's Christmas, and I'm in heaven.

I have several long hairs in my mouth, every body part below my right knee is frozen from the missing covers, and I'm being strangled by the bare arm across my windpipe. And yet—it's by far my favorite way to wake up.

I try to inch over to ease the pressure on my throat. Ragnhild moans in her sleep and snuggles closer. Chills break out all over my body, and for a long second I rethink my stance on oxygen. Do I really need to breathe?

Okay, I do need to breathe. I wrap my fingers around her chilled arm and lift it gently off my neck.

"What are you doing?" Ragnhild's voice is sleepy and soft, her breath warm against my neck. She doesn't move away, instead, she wriggles as if she's trying to get closer—as if that's possible.

"Just ensuring my access to oxygen." I turn my head the slightest bit to kiss her cheek, crinkled with sleep lines from the pillows on my bed. Or maybe from the shoulder seam on my T-shirt. Both possibilities send warmth cascading through my veins.

Her cheek stretches with her smile. "Hi."

"Hi. Do you know what day it is?" I run my fingers along the only part of her back I can reach. Her tank top has slipped up enough to bare a sliver of skin. A sliver that is so warm, so soft under my fingers.

She gasps. "It's *Julaften*! Why aren't you up yet?"

I laugh, but it's more of a croak than anything else. "I can't. In case you haven't noticed, you're quite literally laying on top of me."

She attempts to scramble off, but I wrap my arms around her, tugging her back against me. "I wasn't complaining." I whisper the words into her neck, enjoying the goosebumps racing across her skin.

She holds still for only a moment, then she wriggles in my grasp. "We should get up. I want to see the tree."

This time I let her slip out of my arms and move onto the floor.

Another sharp intake of breath sounds as her feet land on the floorboards. She immediately pulls her feet back up and rubs her upper arms. "How do you live with your floor this freezing?" Her gaze dances around the corners of the room. "Do you have wool socks in here?"

I point to the dresser, and she jumps up and digs around until she finds what she's searching for. The mattress dips as she sits to pull the socks on.

"Come on!" She tugs on the sleeve of my shirt.

I wince as my bare feet hit the floor, but Ragnhild tosses another pair of wool socks at me, and I make quick work of tugging them on. Then we move quietly down the stairs together, both expertly skipping the creaking step halfway down. My mother and Bestemor will sleep for a while longer.

Nerves skip and jump in my stomach. Watching her watch the Christmas tree is my favorite thing, but this year there's even more hinging on this moment.

We tip-toe into the silent, cold backroom and I crawl behind the couch to plug in the tree. In the next moment, the room is lit with the sparkling Christmas tree. I unfold from behind the couch and watch the girl of my dreams.

Her face is bright with awe, reflecting the shining tree before her. Unable to take my eyes off her, I move out from behind the couch.

Her silhouette is outlined by the lit tree as she runs her fingers along the sharp, green needles—reverently touching the sparkling silver tinsel, the strings of tiny Norwegian flags, and the heart-shaped woven paper baskets.

My pulse kicks up as her hand brushes the one in the middle of the tree. Has she seen it yet? She can't have. She has no reason to look inside the thin paper basket, does she?

I step closer, my footfalls loud against the hardwood floors, then muted as I reach the large rug where she stands.

There's no way she hasn't heard me approach, and if she's ignoring me, she must not have seen it. My pulse slows again, a relieved breath slipping past my lips.

Her red hair is longer now, darker than it was when she was little. She's taller, but the wonder on her face mimics the expression she had years ago. A smile pulls at my lips. I'm so happy she hasn't outgrown the tradition of watching the lit tree—I hope she never does.

I close the last step between us, lean close, and whisper into her ear. "You've never lost that expression." She shivers, and I wrap my arms around her, pulling her warm body back against my own.

She turns in my arms. "What expression?"

I run my hands down her bare upper arms, her skin is freezing. "You're cold. Do you need me to get you a blanket?"

She shakes her head even as she snuggles closer into my embrace. "What expression, Thorleif?"

I grin and kiss her nose. My fingers trace the side of her face, her jaw. Her skin is so soft—what if I…. *Focus Thorleif.*

I clear my throat. "When you watch the tree. You used to look just like that as a kid. When we'd sneak down to turn on the tree lights in the mornings."

She smiles. "I remember that." She drops her gaze, cheeks darkening a bit. "It's one of my favorite Christmas traditions."

I nod and bend down to kiss her forehead. "Mine, too."

Then for that other thing. The present I left here before I went upstairs, and that now has my stomach in a vise grip of unease. I swallow down my nerves, drop my hand to her waist again, and tilt my head towards the tree. Why am I so nervous?

I shake my head. That's a ridiculous question. Why wouldn't I be? "There's something in that basket for you."

She doesn't even turn around. Instead, her light eyebrows draw together, scrunching the freckled skin on her nose. She's cute as a button, and I want to kiss that wrinkle between her eyes.

And I will.

In a minute.

Ragnhild is still frowning up at me. "On the tree? What is it?"

I laugh, then press my lips to hers because I can't not. Unsuccessfully, I try to tear myself away. Then again. But she's too intoxicating, too warm and soft and real under my hands.

I kiss the woman of my dreams while the old house creaks as a gust of wind sweeps around the outer walls. The howling wind is loud, but my focus doesn't waver. When I finally pull away my chest is heaving. "You're supposed to look, not ask me what it is."

She still makes no move to turn in my arms, and I suppress a groan. I will never complain about an extra moment with her like this—but just this once, it would be nice if she could follow directions.

But no. Her eyebrows rise, and her chin tips up in challenge. "You know, don't you? So you can just tell me."

I tighten my hands around her waist, relishing the warmth through the thin fabric of her tank top. Why won't she turn? "Of course I know."

"So then tell me."

She snuggles into me, pressing her cold nose into the warm skin of my neck. Goosebumps break out across my skin, but I still manage to shake my head. "No." Short of turning her myself, how do I make her look?

"Please?" She draws the word out in a voice too much like that of the five-year-old I used to know—too much for the question I want to ask her.

"Ragnhild, just turn around and look inside." My voice echoes my exasperation, but I need her to do this herself.

She rolls her eyes, turns, and digs her hand into the heart-shaped paper basket in the middle of the tree. "Fine! If you're going to—"

Her words cut off on a gasp, and she goes very still. The world around us stills, too. The wind quiets down outside, my breath sticks in my lungs, and I don't move. I can't move.

Did I read her all wrong? Is this too much, too soon?

Seconds ago, all I wanted her to do was turn around and see it. Now that she has, all I want is for her to turn back around, but again she refuses to.

Anticipation is a slow and painful death. Will she ever move again?

Then, as if by magic, she does move—turning to me with her mouth open and her blue eyes brimming with tears. She raises her hand between us, holding the simple gold band gingerly between her thumb and pointer finger.

I can't tell what kind of tears these are, not even when one of them slips down her cheek. Are they happy tears? Overwhelmed tears? Or worse, sad tears?

"Does this mean…?" Ragnhild hesitates as if the truth is too tender and fragile to speak out loud. And it is.

I need to ask her the actual question, but I can barely get any words past the chokehold of emotion in my throat. I think…. I think the tears glistening on her cheeks are not sad ones. Maybe over-whelmed ones. Maybe even happy.

When I finally force words across my lips, the ones that emerge aren't the right ones. "You like it?"

She bobs her head up and down, dislodging more shining tears to roll down her cheeks. "I like *you*. Yes."

Happy tears then? My chest loosens a little. "Yes, you like me, or yes, you'll marry me?" I clear my throat again, rushing the words she needs to hear. "Not right now, I know this is brand new, but I want you to know that this is where I want us to go, eventually. This relationship isn't casual for me."

I reach for the ring, drop to one knee, and both her hands clap over her mouth. She blinks furiously, but it's no use. More tears drip down her cheeks, sliding over her freckled nose.

"Will you marry me, Ragnhild? Again?" I add that last word just to see her blush between her tears—and blush she does. A pretty, pink color that spreads into her cheek and down her neck.

She nods again, blue eyes shining with tears, and something else —something I've waited much too long to read in them. Something that looks a lot like forever.

"Yes, I'll marry you." She sniffs, wiping uselessly at her cheeks. "As many times as it takes to stick."

I slip the band onto her finger as laughter rumbles up in my chest. Then I spring to my feet to wrap her back up in my arms. I kiss salty, wet tears off her cheeks. Tears I'm certain are happy ones. "Good."

And there is that expression again—her blue eyes shining with joy. The glow of tree lights and tinsel reflected on a freckled face full of awe. Her smile is brilliant, and her cheeks pink with pleasure as she gazes between the gold band on her finger and the glorious tree, and me. And her eyes on me are everything I've ever wanted.

Because this time the woman I've loved since I was a boy—is finally mine.

CHAPTER 27

RAGNHILD

December 24th, Julaften (Christmas Eve)

I tuck my stockinged feet up under the full black skirts of my *bunad* and lean into the end corner of the couch. The room is warm, and my seat is comfortable, and the view is…. Well, the view of the large man currently digging through the pile of presents at the foot of the glittering Christmas tree is certainly one for the books.

I bite into the side of a thin, crispy gingersnap pig from the abundance of treats on the coffee table. Hazelnuts, walnuts, figs, dates, and the seven types of Christmas cookies required—*smultringer, kokosmakroner, havreflarn, sandnøtter, sirupsnipper, julemenn,* and the gingersnap cookie in my hand. Sweet, spicy crumbs break on my tongue.

Mor Vaage's knitting needles click quietly from the rocking chair by the window, joining the Christmas music streaming throughout the house—and this time there is no mafia affiliate crooning, just the old, sober hymns interspersed with Alf Prøysen's soothing voice. The aroma of our Christmas Eve dinner still lingers in the air—roasted pork and tart sauerkraut mixing with the sweet scent of sauteed apples and prunes.

Thorleif finally stills in his hunt for presents under the green branches of the tree and reaches in for the one he's chosen. He scans the label. Then he springs up from the floor, shaking a flat, soft package in my direction. "This one's for you."

His dark eyes meet mine—his gaze so full of love, of contentment, that it takes effort to look away. He crosses the distance and flops onto the couch next to me—much closer than he sat when he first got up. He hands me the small package and the brush of his fingers sends a million fiery tingles up my arm—like jolts of electricity burrowing under my skin and igniting me from the inside.

My cheeks heat, and my smile feels much too big for my face— too big to keep this wonderful newness between us a secret from the rest of the room. I know we decided to keep the events of this morning quiet longer—we haven't dated more than a few days, and announcing our engagement to Bestemor and Mor Vaage seems way too early.

But even though our actual romantic relationship is newer than the snowy blanket outside, our friendship is old. In some ways, it feels like we've dated our entire lives.

Thorleif grins back at me, his dark eyes sparkling with mirth and drawing mine like magnets. I try not to stare, to not let my gaze wander over this incredible man, but how can I help it?

He left his black wool jacket in the kitchen earlier, and he cuts a handsome figure in only his red vest. With his double row of shiny buttons down his front and billowing linen shirt, he could be a hero stepped right out of a Jane Austen mini-series. Except that, of course, his full beard and wild hair paints a picture far too rugged to be a British gentleman.

My knees turn weak as he lets his gaze wander, too. Dark eyes take me in as if he'll never get enough of just looking. And I hope he doesn't.

My skin aches for his touch. And not the kind that would be appropriate for a Christmas Eve gathering. I push down the delicious sparks that spiral up my spine even as goosebumps break out down my arms. The heat in Thorleif's eyes tells me I'm not the only one wishing we were on our own right now.

I force my eyes to drop from the man next to me down to the wrapped gift in my lap. My fingers shake the tiniest bit as I gently remove the tape from the festive paper. Then my thoughts still completely as the parted sides of the wrapping paper reveal a pair of mittens knit in a traditional Norwegian pattern: two squared black stars on a white background. The wrist cuffs are long with three lines of black. They're what Bestemor calls *Selbuvotter*, mittens from Selbu in Norway.

My voice returns to me with a gasp of delight. "These are beautiful!"

I turn to Mor Vaage, certain the gift must be from her, but she shakes her head. A familiar smile quirks her lips, though. How have I never realized it's exactly the same one Thorleif gives me when he's about to let me in on a secret? But what is Mor Vaage's secret?

I frown. Thorleif didn't knit these mittens—I know that for sure. Surely it's not.... My gaze moves to Bestemor Vaage. Her smiles to me have been stiffer, cooler, ever since I wrote that stupid article, but the smile she sends me now cannot be called either. No, this one is soft and warm. And her eyes sparkle like they used to before my article entered the world wide web to wreak havoc on her family's reputation.

Tears well in my eyes as I break her gaze to inspect my gift closer. I blink quickly, clearing the moisture from my eyes, and lift the mittens again to admire the crisscross pattern on the back.

I scrunch my brows when I get to the second mitten. It isn't the same size as the first. It looks nothing like the diamond-shaped mitten I first saw—this one is larger and rounded. If I'd attempted to knit a pair of mittens, I might have ended up with something like this. But Bestemor has knit mittens for her family for longer than I've been alive. If hers is shaped like this it must be on purpose.

I pick up the ballooned mitten. Is that a third mitten underneath it? "What are these?" I don't want to sound ungrateful, but I'm so confused.

Bestemor's eyes twinkle at me, and her gaze moves to Thorleif. Her attention drops to the shrinking number of inches between the two of us. She winks at Thorleif, and I catch the darkening of his cheekbones. Then her attention is on me again. *"Kjærestevotter."*

The word is Norwegian, that much I know, but what does it mean? I glance at Thorleif. He still looks slightly embarrassed, but he grins at me. The twinkle in his eyes matches Bestemor and Mor Vaage's. Because I'm the only one in this room who doesn't know what I've just received.

Thorleif clears his throat. "Girlfriend mittens."

I still as his words swirl in my mind, wreaking havoc on my composure. Girlfriend mittens? If he hadn't already asked me to marry him, this would be the strangest determine-the-relationship conversation I've ever had—in front of his mother and grand-mother, no less. But though I know the depth of his feelings for me, it doesn't change the warmth blooming in my heart over him all but calling me his girlfriend. We didn't talk about terms, but if our end goal is marriage, surely we're at least that.

Thorleif shakes his head, grinning down into his lap. "No, there's a better translation." He frowns as he contemplates his next words. "More like sweetheart mittens."

My pulse skitters ever faster as he looks over at me. But I still don't know what that means. "Sweetheart mittens? What on earth is that?"

Thorleif's deep laugh rumbles next to me, and all I want is to close the last few inches between us and curl up next to him—to be as close as possible to that laugh, and him. In his lap if possible.

And maybe Christmas magic is real because he motions for me to move closer. "C'mere, I'll show you."

I don't have a chance to move before he does, sliding so close our elbows are touching, and he has to be sitting on top of my full skirts. He grabs the bigger mitten and puts it on his left hand, then points to the smallest one. "Put that one on your right hand."

"This mitten"—he points to the ballooned knit piece that doesn't look like a mitten at all—"has two wrist openings. One for each of us."

Thorleif slides his hand into the giant double-mitten at the same time as I do. His large, warm hand wraps around mine inside the roomy knit pocket. I shift my fingers so I can lace them between his. And incredibly enough, there's room for me to do so. Sparks tingle in my fingertips, and from the bob of his Adam's apple, I think he feels it, too.

His voice is only a tad thicker than usual when he speaks. "It's for hand-holding in cold weather." He winks at me, and the butterflies behind my ribs start up again. I slept in his arms last night, but knowing he wants to hold my hand still does funny things to my insides. Then I remember who made the gift.

I turn towards Bestemor. Is this a peace offering? It must be, right?

I swallow. I don't know how to ask her if she can ever forgive me, not when my words are so small and trite in comparison to the hurt I caused her. But what if this gift is a sign that she has already? Or, at least, that she's trying to? The hours of work this must have taken her. Is that the reason she's left the room so often when I've walked in? Not because she couldn't stand my presence?

Stormy emotions well up in my chest, and my voice refuses to come. Instead, tears fill my eyes, making Bestemor's face blur across the room.

I pull my hand out of Thorleif's and from our shared mitten. Freeing my skirts out from under his legs, I rise from the couch. Three quick steps across the floor, and I lean down to wrap my arms tightly around Bestemor. She smells like perfume, summer, and sunscreen—even in December. I've always secretly wished she was my grandmother. And her tight hug makes me hope she feels the same.

I let my arms fall to my sides, but Bestemor stands and folds me into a hug even tighter than the first. Tears trail down both our cheeks, and I whisper my thanks.

I repeat the words in Norwegian. *"Tusen takk."*

"Værsågod." You're welcome.

I don't know how she could have possibly known what was going on between me and Thorleif long enough to finish this project. Our conscious relationship is just days old. But maybe she knew we were supposed to be together the same way Thorleif did. Maybe Bestemor Vaage saw all the little signs I refused to for so long.

If so, is this gift more than a peace offering? Is it also a welcome to her family?

I can't know that for sure. But I hope so.

CHAPTER 28

THORLEIF

The night is over. The dishes sit drying in the dish rack in the kitchen. The leftovers from our Christmas Eve dinner have been put away, and piles of wrapping paper and ribbons no longer litter the floor around the Christmas tree.

The older generations have found their beds, leaving the younger one in charge of unplugging Christmas lights and blowing out candles before settling down, too.

After perhaps a kiss or two.

Judging by the congratulations I received from both Bestemor and my mother, I'm no longer certain it's possible to keep secrets in this house. Neither of them should know about my proposal. But maybe their wide smiles were only because they think we're together, not that we're also engaged?

Leaving only the one Tiffany table lamp glowing, I shut the door to the living room. The backroom is dark apart from the sparkling Christmas tree. But it's much warmer than it was this morning since I placed the space heater in here for Christmas Eve.

Ragnhild stands by the tree. She touches each ornament, each strand of tinsel—lost in her own little dream world. Just like when she was a little girl.

But when she hears my heavy footfalls, she lifts her head and drops her hand from the tinsel. I step closer and wrap my arms around her, leaning my chin on her shoulder.

She giggles, then tries, and fails, to close the gap between her jaw and shoulder. I nuzzle closer and the giggles turn to laughter. "Your beard tickles."

She wriggles, and I loosen my hold on her just a little. She turns in my arms, heavy skirts swishing and the silver brooch on her chest jingling. My fingers play with the thick embroidered belt around her waist, and I tighten my hold on her, feeling the warmth of her body even through the layers of her bunad.

She pushes up on her toes and presses a quick kiss to my mouth. "I missed you."

I raise my eyebrows. "I've been here all day." But I've missed her, too.

She shrugs. "Not like this." No, it's certainly not been quite like this.

I hold her tight to me, whispering into her hair. "Did you have a good *Julaften?*"

She nods. "The best. How about you?"

"I got everything I wanted for Christmas."

She pulls back a bit, enough to meet my gaze. "What was it you wanted for Christmas?"

I lean forward and kiss her lips softly. "Isn't that obvious?"

Her lips stretch into a smile under mine. "Did you want new mittens?"

I laugh, but she cuts it off with a kiss. I pull away, dropping one on her nose instead. "No, Ragnhild. I wanted this. You."

And now tears shine in her eyes. "I can't say I wanted you, but I'm so glad I got you."

I kiss the single tear off her cheek and press my stubbly one against hers. "Me, too, Ragnhild. Me, too."

CHAPTER 29

RAGNHILD

Julaften morning (Christmas Eve), one year later

Julemorgen, Christmas Eve morning, arrives with a quiet snowfall outside the window of our second-floor apartment. I'm warm and snug as a bug wrapped up in a down comforter next to my brand-new husband.

I open my eyes to the bright light of a December morning outside the bedroom window, and the heavy weight of Thorleif's arm slung over my waist.

Our bedroom isn't very big, but it's big enough for what matters —like the Christmas tree that stands fully decorated across the room and ready for lighting. The green branches support long lines of sparkling tinsel, strings with tiny Norwegian flags, and several angry-eyed felt ornaments Thorleif and I made as children.

I've never had a Christmas tree in my bedroom before, but this year there was no question of where it should go.

Thorleif and I stayed up late last night decorating it together. Truth be told, there was probably significantly more kissing than decorating happening—hence the late night. Newlyweds aren't necessarily the most efficient tree decorators. But we already knew that from trying to decorate Bestemor and Mor Vaage's tree earlier that day.

Thorleif stirs behind me, and happiness spreads like the warmth of a million Christmas lights in my chest. I can't believe he's mine—can't believe I worked so hard to keep him at a distance last December.

He makes a contented noise behind me as his arm tightens, tugging me closer with his grip on my waist. Soon he nuzzles his nose into my neck, and his soft beard tickles my skin. Sparks of electricity light under my skin, and I can hardly believe this is my life now.

Thorleif coughs and shakes his head with a sputtering noise. His other hand reaches up to move my hair and the strands that found their way into his mouth. It's not an uncommon problem. As usual, it makes me laugh—and he growls in response.

And I don't mind that at all.

But I do take pity on him and turn in his arms to kiss him good morning. And the frown on his beautiful face disappears as his lips tug in a smile he can't hold back. And once he's lost the battle, he laughs and rolls us over so he can deliver his own good morning kisses. Sizzling, warm, perfect kisses.

After more than a few minutes, we break apart. Newlyweds are apparently also quite terrible at getting their day started in an efficient manner.

Not that I'd want it any other way.

"You ready?" Thorleif's whisper is warm against my ear, and we both scramble to a seated position on the bed. There's no need to venture downstairs this year, but I'm still dreading the few steps we'll have to take across the cold floor to plug in the lights.

Instead of scooting to the end of the bed, Thorleif pulls me back into his arms so my back is flush against his chest. I'm not going to complain about that, so I settle in. The Christmas tree can wait, I guess.

But Thorleif's one arm wraps around me, and then…the Christmas tree lights up.

The tinsel glitters, the lights glow, and the ornaments sparkle. My chest warms and my heart feels light, and even though I saw it fully decorated last night, it still takes my breath away.

But…. I frown and turn to my husband. "Thorleif! How did it just light on its own?"

He grins, eyes dancing as he keeps me in suspense. Then he kisses my mouth, lingering so long I almost forget my question. Almost.

I pull back, struggling to put my frown back on my face. Thankfully, only raised eyebrows are needed to make him answer. He holds up his other hand, a tiny black box in his grip. "The lights have a remote."

I frown as I pull my gaze away from Thorleif and back to the Christmas tree in all its shining glory. I wasn't aware that we had anything but regular old Christmas lights. "I thought you were old-fashioned and wanted to turn them on manually for me?"

He pulls me tighter, and even though this is not new anymore, my cheeks still flush. His breath is warm against my ear. "Yeah. Well, that was before. When I needed to go downstairs to see you."

He presses a kiss behind my ear, and goosebumps break out all over my skin. We've been married for three days, and I can't get enough of him—of this. I don't know if I ever will.

"And now?" My voice doesn't sound remotely like my own, but how can it when my new husband is trailing warm, lingering kisses down my neck? I tilt my head, giving him better access and he murmurs his appreciation.

"Now I prefer to stay in bed. So I can kiss you properly."

And quite frankly, I do, too.

Even more so when he tugs at the neckline of my Christmas pajamas shirt, leaving my shoulder bare. The air in the room is cold since the heat has yet to kick on. But Thorleif doesn't give my bare skin a second to feel the chill before his mouth is there making good on his promise.

His beard is soft against my collarbone, and this is by far my favorite Christmas morning ever. His hands move down to my hips, settling there with firm conviction. Conviction that's also in his voice, has always been in his voice. "I love you, Ragnhild."

I close my eyes, needing to feel his touch, the warmth of his words, his calloused fingers on my skin, more than I need to see our Christmas tree.

The shining lights are still bright against the backs of my eyelids, and the room is cool as my best friend tugs me close against his warm chest. And the strongest, safest hands I know slide over my bare stomach. "I love you, too, Thorleif."

His hands move again, and….

Oh. My. Gosh.

THE END

Keep reading for an excerpt from my enemies to lovers fantasy romance, A Winter Proposal.

Find out what I'm writing next by signing up for my newsletter here: www.authoraustinryan.com

Please consider leaving a review on Amazon or Goodreads, so I can keep writing the stories in my heart. It really does help!

EXCERPT — A WINTER PROPOSAL

Chapter 1

The Northwoods,
Twenty days before the winter solstice

I once was a girl who believed in magic.

Faeries and trolls were as real to me as the dancing colors in the night skies above our cabin. The stories my grandmother told by the glowing hearth fueled my imagination until I saw traces of magic everywhere. I saw faerie folk dancing in the sparkle of drifting snow, felt their power in my grandmother's soothing touch, their irreverence in the brook's laugh through the ice. But when the woman who loved me like a daughter died, my childish beliefs had done nothing to save me from the cruelty that followed.

Sitting on the frozen stone steps, the chill seeps through my wool skirts, pressing the cold winter day into my skin. I pull my shawl tighter around my shoulders.

Across from me and down the road, scattered log cabins are draped in winter darkness. Snow blankets the slanted roofs and stone slab steps in the little town I've called home for just a quarter of my life.

Muddy sleigh tracks and hoof marks sparkle with frost, and the shiny layers of ice catch the flickering glow from torches held aloft by housefolk moving quietly between outbuildings.

It's been almost a decade since my grandmother died now. And still, her presence feels no further away than the stars winking down at me from the velvety darkness above. The quiet of early morning stretches around me, even if it looks like night—we're too far north for the sun to rise for hours yet.

My grandmother's laughing voice sounds in my ear, flavored by the lilt from her island roots. "For our endless summer nights, we pay a steep price in winter, Saoirse."

She wasn't wrong. Most days, the little daylight I see is through the windows of the Pedersen's main house, while I scrub floors and empty night pots. If I'm lucky I'll catch a bit of sunset when extra hands are needed for the afternoon milking.

A creak erupts in the stillness, pulling me out of my thoughts. A tabby cat pushes through my neighbor's half-shut door and slinks away down the path between our two cabins.

I shiver as the memories of my grandmother inevitably morph into the memories of after she died. Faded images of my life with the aunt who took me in flash through my mind, twisting their blades painfully in my chest.

I shoot up from the steps and stomp into the alley as if memories like these can be outrun. But if there's a chance—I'll give it my all.

Silver-frosted grass crunches under my boots as I follow the tabby down the alley between the two cabins. I'm desperate to escape both the ache in my chest and the prying eyes of my neighbors. Will the solitude in the hollow of naked, frostbitten trees down the hill from our cabin be enough? It will have to be.

The dark-striped tabby is merely a shadow as it pounces on thin air, streaks across icicle grass, and is swallowed by the snow-laden vines.

My boots scrape the frozen ground just like the grief does my raw heart. My grandmother's stories shimmer and clatter in the cold air the same way her laughter once did between the buildings.

The darkness pooling in the shadows makes my imagination run wild.

Soon, I'm eleven again, seated at her knee by our hearthfire as her stories fill the air, twisting and curling like the sharp smoke tickling my nose. Her warm hand rests on my shoulder as she tells me of *Huldra*, the beautiful cow-tailed faerie woman luring young men down into the mountain—never to be seen again.

Her eyes hold mine as she warns me:

Never trust the faeries, Saoirse, they know no other way than deceit.

Gooseflesh prickles down my spine as I remember her story of the farmer who refused to pay the faerie taking care of his animals, only for it to kill off all the farmer's livestock. Another about a faerie dancing a servant girl to death for stealing the promised lump of butter from his porridge.

Don't try to bargain with the magic folk.

Other stories spin through my mind, no more flattering of the faeries than the ones before. But for all her warnings, I'd still believed the magic folk was more than evil faeries. Surely those faeries who danced in the ribbons of light in the night skies would save my grandmother when she fell ill? Didn't faeries know the secrets of life and death? Didn't they have healing magic?

For weeks I kept my eyes peeled for striking tree stumps or a darkened hollow, ready to strike whatever bargain needed to heal her.

But the faeries never came.

And when I was sent to an aunt I'd never met, I waited with bated breath for the magic folk to find me. Surely they were just delayed?

Their magic would save me from the bruising force of her anger, wouldn't it?

I'd run away from my aunt the first chance I'd gotten, long after I'd realized that the faeries would never come. Because they didn't exist. My grandmother's stories had been just that—stories.

And while lights still dance in the skies over my home, there is no magic in it. The sparkles in drifting snow are just the reflection of sunlight. The laughing brook only trapped water. And my grandmother's love died with her.

Blood seeps freshly from a wound over ten years old, and I press my hand against my heart as if I can still the flow from the outside. But there's no use.

I wipe away the moisture on my cold cheeks as the cat crawls ghostlike out from the brambles. Did it catch its prey already?

I crouch down to call it when a flash of bright light stings my eyes, and my voice freezes in my throat.

When I blink my eyes open, the cat is gone.

In its place is a man whose snow-white shirt sleeves are a sharp contrast to his dark waistcoat and the breeches tucked into tall boots.

The air in my lungs turns to ice as I try to comprehend what my eyes are telling me. He can't possibly be what I think he is, can he? Faeries were ugly in my grandmother's stories, repulsive to the humans who crossed their paths. Only when they wanted a human's favor did they possess ethereal beauty—like the cow-tailed woman or the faeries who swapped human children for their ugly changelings.

But this man, with his sharp jaw and high cheekbones, smooth, golden skin, and full lips? Ethereal is the only way to describe this man.

No human could look this perfect.

And no human could transform from a cat to a man in a flash of light, Saoirse!

My mouth goes dry as I spot the most damning evidence of all—certain those are pointed ears sticking out of his hair.

I hold my breath as each and every childhood story swirls inside my head until bile tickles the back of my throat.

Faeries don't exist. They are stories, Saoirse. Folklore, faerie tales, fiction.

But while I was once happy to embellish my grandmother's stories, to let the faeries be kind to humans, I know those were only the fantasies of an innocent child. If faeries *are* real, they must be like my grandmother told me—unpredictable and conniving, without regard for human life.

I shudder soundlessly in the dark, not daring to move a muscle.

The man sighs deeply and removes a dagger from the leather sheath at his waist.

No.

Not the man. *The faerie.*

The blade in his hand, sharp-edged and deadly, catches the faint light from the snow, and my stomach sinks further. I have nowhere to hide in this barren winter landscape, and the eerie half-light in this hollow will be no match for a faerie's sharp vision. If he turns even slightly, he'll see me.

Fear holds breath captive in my chest.

A faerie would think nothing of killing a human, and I have just seen this one shift from a cat to a man. What will he do once he realizes I know his secret?

My heart thrashes against my ribcage, thundering so loudly he *must* hear it.

I need to run, to at least try to escape. But as much as my legs ache to get me out of here, what is the use? The faerie will only halt me in my tracks with a flick of his wrist.

I close my eyes, and ragged breaths saw in and out of my lungs as I wait for him to see me. To kill me.

Time drags on as I wait for the end, but nothing happens.

When I finally open my eyes, the man, faerie—whatever he was —is gone.

Chapter 2

I run from the hollow to the cabin, legs moving faster than they have in my life. Terror nips at my heels, claws at my heart, seeps into my bones. With every booming heartbeat, hands pull at my skirts, my hair. Strong, tanned hands wielding a sharp blade, ready to take my life away from me.

My heart and lungs are close to bursting when I finally cross the threshold, into the warmth and light from the hearth. I slam the door shut on the silvery winter night outside, and sink to the floor.

Ingerid's dark skirts swirl around her bare ankles as she jumps away from the simmering pot in the hearth. Her hand slaps to her chest. "You startled me!"

But then she gets a better look at me propped up against the door jamb, gasping for breath, and she frowns. "Are you all right, Saoirse?"

I try to answer, but my teeth chatter too much. How do you tell someone you've seen a faerie?

It takes several deep breaths before I gain control over my voice, and even then, I stumble over my words. "I saw a tabby cat, but it wasn't... I mean, it looked like a faerie, and I thought. I closed my eyes and—"

Ingerid tosses her honey-blonde braid back over her shoulder, and sighs. "Do you think maybe you fell asleep out there?"

Did I?

"Yes... I think I must have." Relief trickles through me as I clamp onto the explanation with a desperation fit to the terror still pounding through my veins. The three of us stayed up too late last night—I must have dozed off on the steps, that's all.

It was a nightmare. Only a nightmare.

Of course there wasn't a faerie in the hollow, Saoirse. You were thinking of how much you missed your grandmother, and then you dreamed about her faerie stories.

It's been so long since her death, but I don't think I'll ever be rid of the ache. Especially not on these dark winter mornings that remind me of her.

"It sounds like it was a rough one. How about I warm some honey milk for you?" Ingerid pushes the porridge pot to the side of the hearth, already reaching for the smaller pot hanging from the hooks above the fire.

I nod, and my hand barely shakes as I pull out the bench tucked under the table where three wooden bowls sit ready for breakfast.

At twenty-two, Ingerid is barely a year older than me. None of us have ever known our parents, but it's never stopped Ingerid from taking on the task of mothering Liisa and me. I never would have made it through my first night alone in the Northwoods if she hadn't shared her hiding place with me, nor would Liisa, if we hadn't found her that same night.

I gulp down the honey milk and let its warmth spread beneath my breastbone and into my veins. Slowly, it banishes the terror in my bones. By the time Liisa stumbles into the room, looking more dead than alive, I feel almost like myself again.

My youngest found sister staggers to the table—her thick, dark hair still a mess from sleep. "I need to go to the smithy—" Her words are cut off by a yawn and the scraping sound as she pulls out her end of the bench and dumps herself onto it. She rubs her eyes as if she's much younger than her twenty years.

"The blacksmith?" Ingerid turns a sly gaze on me as she joins us at the table, flicking her braid out of reach of her porridge bowl. "Why don't you have Saoirse run your errand? She needs to go there, too."

This is news to me. "I do?"

Ingerid's grin is bright in the flickering light, and mirth dances in her eyes. "Yes, you do." She almost sings the words, but I'm still confused.

Across the table, Liisa shoves a spoonful of porridge into her mouth as if it can stop her next yawn. It doesn't, but when the yawn lets go of her, she nods to me. "You can go for me, Saoirse, but what are you doing there?"

"I'm… not sure?" I look to Ingerid for an explanation.

Her eyes widen, then she huffs. "Not something. *Someone*, Saoirse."

My cheeks heat as I catch her meaning.

Liisa and I serve at the Pedersen farm for the use of this old cabin, and Ingerid's long days at Erkki's father's farm keep us in food. But when the blacksmith's son shaved off those awful sideburns at the end of last winter, I realized what I should have long ago—that three orphaned girls can't live on their own forever.

We'll have to marry and find homes of our own sooner rather than later. And Ask, especially sans sideburns, is a fine choice for a husband.

Ingerid smirks, pausing her spoon halfway to her mouth as she reaches for the red butter dish. "He won't ask you to be his wife if he never sees you, will he?"

"I guess not?" I pull in a deep breath, and the excitement tingling in my chest melds with the comfort of the honey milk. Just for a moment, the warmth and safety of my grandmother's hearth feels within reach again. *A real home.*

"He won't." She plops a pat of butter onto her porridge, and the yellow lump is like a warning bell. Ask's lopsided smile fades in my mind's eye, and the terror of this morning floods my veins. Would the faerie I saw in the hollow kill for a stolen butter lump?

Faeries don't exist, Saoirse, remember? You don't believe in magic.

I close my eyes and steady my breaths, trying to calm my thundering heart. But it's no use, because no matter what I told Ingerid, and tried to tell myself, I know what I saw.

And as I later strap on my wooden skis to trek through the winter darkness for another day of endless scrubbing of clothes and floors at the Pedersen farm, my grandmother's stories swirl in my head.

They never scared me as a child. Armed with the love that always surrounded me, the cruel behavior of the faeries was no worry of mine. But as I recall the stories now, each one is more terrifying than the one before.

Not because I'm no longer a child—but because they are no longer stories.

Chapter 3

Spruce trees, tall and heavy with snow, stand sentinel along the path as I ski home through the woods. Changelings' pained cries carry on the wind, and a tendril of fear snakes through my chest. Soon, a hulking troll looms in my periphery, and I whip my head around, catching my breath as the terror rattles my heart.

But no, it's not a troll, just the same snowladen boulder I pass every night.

I stop and stab my long ski pole into a snow bank. With my hands free, I tighten the shawl around my shoulders. Then I pick my pole back up, put my grandmother's stories out of my head, and hasten my speed.

But the memories of the magic I saw as a child won't leave me alone. Not now that I've admitted to myself that my faerie sighting wasn't a nightmare.

Because if the magic folk were real all this time, why didn't they save me?

I was a child—I deserved to be saved.

But I already know why, even as her voice echoes once again. *Because the faeries cannot be trusted, child.*

Minutes later, I unstrap my skis, and lean them up against the side of the cabin. I knock my boots against the steps, and—as the caked-on snow falls off—open the door.

I've had no more encounters with magical beings in the two days since I saw the faerie in the hollow. Unless I count the shiny eyes flashing from my neighbor's stone steps as I returned that night. The memory of the cat's unnerving attention has goosebumps spreading across my shoulders even now. Thankfully, it's nowhere to be seen as I lift the latch and go inside. I pull off my shawl, hood, and mittens, and rub my arms for warmth.

The mending basket filled with red and blue stockings sits ready for me on the table, and my sigh is a plume of white smoke in front of my face. After preparing a cup of steaming coffee, I sit down and pull the first of Liisa's stockings into my lap. An hour later, the basket seems as bottomless as when I started.

A barrage of filthy words, loud enough to penetrate the thick window glass, pulls me out of my thoughts. A horse whinnies wildly, and a child cries.

Drawn by the ache in my chest at that last sound, I push open the door. The frame groans as if what I'm about to see won't be to my liking.

And it isn't.

Resting my cheek against the cold door post, I try to make sense of the scene in front of me.

The brightly painted sleigh stopped on the road screams of its owner's wealth. As does the driver in his heavy fur coat, poisoning the air with profanities directed at the crowd by the side of the road. But a sleigh this fine is not a common sight in this small North-woods town, and I don't blame them for staring.

The driver's whip whistles through the air as he takes his rage out on the team of onyx horses. One of them rears up. Ears flat against its head, its powerful hooves cut through the air before it returns to the ground with a thundering sound. A little girl squeals and presses into her mother's dark skirts.

The cries that first pulled me out here, turn to a wail, and I search for the source.

My neighbor, a handsome man if not for the angry grimace twisting his features, has one meaty fist hooked into his little boy's collar as he hauls him away from the edge of the street.

Big tears stream down the child's red face. "I didn't run into the road!"

The man's snarls are too low to hear over the still cursing sleigh driver and the chatter of the crowd, but the boy winces. Still he wrenches free from the man's grip and fists his small hands on his hips. "I need to get my cat, you don't understand! He saved me from getting hit!"

"If I see that cat again, I'll kill it myself, do you hear me?" He tosses a glance in the direction of the stomping horses. "It's as good as dead already."

Another sob from the boy twists my stomach. He throws a last look towards the street where the driver is still trying to control the horses, and the heartache etched on his face is too much. His pleading eyes catch mine, and I can't look away.

"Please, my cat." His words aren't directed at the sorry excuse of a man pushing him towards the tarred cabin next to mine. They are directed at me.

Cold settles in my stomach as I move out of the doorway, jump off the stone steps, and sprint towards the road. I make my way through the small crowd until my nostrils fill with the filthy stench seeping through the ice broken by the stomping hooves.

I blink and strain my neck to catch a glimpse of the boy's cat. There, under the sleigh is a dark shape in the slushy mixture of snow and mud. Its striped fur is darkened with blood, but I'm certain it's the boy's cat.

Except, it isn't truly that.

Fear swirls in my stomach as terror dances through my memories of that morning in the hollow. Surely it's the same creature that shifted into a faerie? What good could possibly come from saving it?

"Better just end its miserable life!" From the side of the road, my irate neighbor shouts the words I can't deny are in my own heart.

The boy howls, a door slams, and they're gone.

Compassion stirs in my heart, but can I truly save the life of this creature, knowing what it is? But what if the boy was right and this faerie saved him from being run over?

Faeries don't save children, Saoirse. You know that better than anyone.

And I do.

After all, I have the scars to prove it.

The sleigh inches forward with a loud groan, the runners about to cross right over the animal's spine. Not pausing to think, I throw myself forward. "Please stop, sir! You'll kill it!"

But heedless of my cries, the sleigh shudders away over the uneven road with a sickening crunch. The driver's ugly curses are too faint to penetrate the haze in my brain as bile rises in my throat. I clamp my hand over my mouth, certain I'll hurl at the sight about to meet me. Dipping my head, I search the muddle of snow where the sleigh passed and glimpse lumps of bloodied fur. I shudder, and look away.

But while I might not mourn the life of an evil faerie, the little boy's pleading eyes won't let me leave the animal he loved out here to be tossed about like trash. *Faerie or not.*

I kneel in the frozen mud, bracing for the touch of lifeless flesh. The metallic scent of blood fills my nostrils, and I hold my breath. Pressing my hand against the icy ground, I scoop the feline up, cradling it gently. Its body is still warm, and fresh blood soaks the dark sleeves of my jacket. And then...

It moves.

Not a spasm, but real movement.

It's alive.

I gasp as fear wars with hope inside me—I'm holding a living faerie in my arms!

Thundering hooves and swishing runners sound again, and I barely manage to jump out of the way as another sleigh rushes past me.

Scandalized whispers reach my ears. "What is she doing with the dead cat? It doesn't belong to her, does it?" A woman I don't know leans forward to glare at me.

"Look at the state of her dress!" Kari Bakken clutches her little sister's hand as she sweeps a glare of disdain over my soiled clothes.

I roll my eyes. A little boy was almost hit by a sleigh and they care about the state of my clothes? But my problems are bigger than that right now. I need to get the faerie, cat, whatever it is, inside—away from the prying eyes of the crowd before it shifts. Can it still shift?

The shivering body stirs in my arms, and I quicken my steps, careful to avoid the icy patches.

My neighbors tip their heads together, and their whispers are like a buzz on the air. All eyes are on my stained dress and the bloodied lump in my arms. But the only set of eyes I care about are those in the tearstained face pressed against the thick window glass of the cabin next to mine.

Finally, I push my door open, letting out a breath of relief as it creaks shut behind me. One-handed, I spread a clean linen towel on the table.

Liisa doesn't often return before dark, and Ingerid won't be home until after dinner. The sun rose not long ago, so there are several hours left of daylight. Can I tend to the cat and return it to the boy before either of the girls come home?

But as I look at the barely breathing creature in my arms, I know there's no way—it's too badly injured. I lower the cat onto the table, remove my filthy jacket, and unbutton my wrists to shove my now stained shirt sleeves to my elbows.

The crunching sound of the runners sliding over the animal's back plays on repeat in my mind, and a violent shudder shakes my shoulders.

Its spine *must* be broken—it shouldn't have survived the heavy sleigh, and yet, its warm belly rises and falls under my hands. Because of its magic?

But couldn't a magical faerie have evaded the sleigh in the first place?

I try not to think of what I'm really doing as I cleanse the deep lacerations across the cat's back. The water in the basin turns more pink for each swirl of my cloth. I wring it out, again and again, until I'm certain the wounds are as clean as I can get them.

Keeping an eye on the table, I rifle through a chest for Ingerid's healing salve. I pull the waxed fabric off the pot, and breathe in the scent of sunshine and honey, thankful for a reprieve from my nasty task. Dabbing the sticky salve at the broken skin along the cat's back, I tie another linen strip around it. Then I repeat the process along its silky underside.

One more swipe of my finger through the velvety contents of the tin, and I spread it across the last scrape. The striped fur grows warm, then smooths under my fingers. I hold my breath as its color darkens and the markings fade.

The sudden appearance of smooth, golden skin is the only warning I get as the air cracks and a flash of lighting blinds me.

A limb is shoved into my stomach.

A string of dark curses fill the room. And then, I'm staring into frosty green eyes.

Faeries aren't real.

The faerie's gaze drops, and I follow it to where my hands are clutching his warm waist. His *bare* waist, save for the strips of bandages.

Heat rushes to my cheeks as I pull my hands off his skin and back away from his knee. His bottom half—*thank God!*—is covered by the dark cloth of his breeches.

"No need to move your hands on my account." Even slurred, his melodious voice tugs at something behind my ribs, flooding my body with heat. His smirk is more than suggestive, and I open my mouth to retort when another crack sounds.

I shield my eyes from the sharp flash about to follow.

But there's no light, only more curses, and when I drop my hand, the faerie is on the floor—the broken pieces of our table sticking out from under him.

Fear chills my stomach as he pushes to his feet and his hazy eyes meet mine. He sways, and another weak curse escapes him as his face grows even paler. Then his eyes roll back in his head, and he crumples into the broken table.

The crack of the surface slab splinters the air, and I wince, but the faerie doesn't stir.

I stand frozen as bright daylight streams into the room from the window by the door, illuminating the unbelievable scene in front of me. A half-naked, wounded faerie on top of our broken table.

I pull in a weak breath, and settle trembling fists on my hips.

I might need to amend my own belief in magical beings, and question why I thought they'd come for me. But if my grandmother's tales are true, I can't expose my sisters to this danger. What if Ingerid comes home early?

I'll need to find a way to hide him away until I can decide what to do—except, how on earth does one hide a faerie? Especially one so large?

He needs to wake up.

I tap his leg with the toe of my boot.

His build might be lithe compared to Ask's, but he's still both taller and wider than me, and I won't be able to move him on my own.

I bend to give his warm shoulder a shove. "Wake up!"

He whimpers, but his eyes stay closed. Strips of linen cover the worst of his wounds and I've applied the sticky honey-salve to the rest of them, but he's still mostly naked. And there's no way I can move him without touching him.

I groan.

Move him? Where on earth will I move him? I have no chance of getting him upstairs, but where else is there?

I yell at him a few more times, but I don't dare touch him again.

Pulling my wide sleeves to my wrists, leaving as little skin exposed as possible, I bend and wrap my arms around his torso. His shoulders jam up under my chin, and his clean-shaven face is much too close to mine. Dark blonde hair brushes my temple, and my skin pebbles. His skin is smooth and warm under my hands, against my cheek. *No it isn't. He's a faerie!*

Droplets of sweat trickle down my back as I pull him off the broken table pieces and across the threshold to the rough hewn slabs of wood leading upstairs.

He groans, and startled by the sound, I almost drop him. As I resettle my grip, his eyes are still closed, his body still dead weight in my arms. I don't let my gaze linger on the smooth muscles of his stupid abdomen. *Faerie, not ogling material.*

The stairs to the second floor have never been so steep, or so long. I make it up two steps before I need a break. I hope faeries don't bruise easily, because I have no way of preventing the backs of his calves from hitting every single step as I haul him upwards.

Halfway up, my hands are slick with sweat, and I lose my grip. He slides down my body until his face is no longer next to mine, but halfway down my torso.

He moans and turns his face, practically smashing it into my heaving chest. "Ey, how did I get here? I like this."

Oh God, I'm going to combust from embarrassment.

He makes no move to stand, and I refasten my grip around the upper part of his torso, pulling him away from my chest.

"Where are you taking me, my heart?"

He did *not* just call me that. But though his words are slurred and he can't know who he's talking to, my heart gives a little jolt at the endearment. A jolt I immediately shut down. "I can't have you passed out on our broken table."

"Am I your... scandalous... little secret?" There's no mistaking the flirtatious tone this time.

I ignore him, groaning as I heft him up another step, and suddenly his face is so close to mine. Too close. His eyelashes flutter against my cheek. "Oh, I like this even more."

"Well, you're the only one. I don't like this at all." I grind out the words, cursing whoever first decided second floors were needed.

The faerie's lips brush my jaw, and I can't tell if it's an accident or not.

Of course it's an accident, Saoirse.

"You don't like me?" His breath is warm against my neck. "I'm pretty sure you're supposed to like me." His voice is pouty, like that of a little boy not getting his way.

I roll my eyes. "And *I'm* pretty sure you need to lay off the butter on your porridge. You're—" I grunt as I heave him up one more step. "Too heavy."

He tsks. "Maybe you need to get a bit stronger, little human."

An answer is on the tip of my tongue, but then he goes limp in my arms. Again. When I get a look at his face, his eyes are closed and his lips parted.

I wish I was the one passed out, rather than the one needing to pull a full-grown man the rest of the way to my room. If faeries had to be real, couldn't they at least have been a little lighter?

MORE BOOKS BY AUSTIN RYAN

TALES FROM THE NORTHWOODS SERIES

A Winter Proposal, An Enemies to Lovers Romance (Book 1)
A Traveller Bargain (Book 2) Coming 2024

THE TRIANGLE OF SPIRITS SERIES

Pirate's Treasure (Book 1)
Mermaid's Tale (Book 2) Coming 2024

STAND ALONES

The Fairshaw Library, A Victorian Gaslamp Fantasy Romance
The Christmas Marriage Plot, A Norwegian Heritage Novella (an earlier version of this story)

AUTHOR'S NOTE

The Christmas Marriage Plot was the first book I wrote. It started as a 1500-word piece of flash fiction that turned into a 13,000-word novella, filled with all the Christmas traditions from my upbringing in Norway and my love of farm boys in flannel shirts. When I published it in 2020, my grandfather had just passed away seven weeks earlier, and I'd hoped to present it to my grandmother as a Christmas gift.

The day after my book was published she suffered an injury she would never recover from, and died a week later, the day before Christmas Eve.

I love the original novella I wrote in the fall of 2020, and I have no plans to unpublish it in its current form. But I realized there was more story to dig into, and this full-length novel is the result of that (figurative) creative digging.

The change from third person past to first person present is simply to reflect my best writing voice and to match my other books. I believe I've stayed true to the feel of the original characters and story, and I hope you love it as much as I do.

I also added a long-requested pronunciation guide for the main characters' Norwegian names and a list of definitions of the Norwegian words sprinkled throughout the story.

As always, thank you for taking the time to read this little piece of my heart—I sincerely hope you've enjoyed it!

- Austin

ACKNOWLEDGMENTS

In John Donne's words, no man is an island (and no woman is either)—so many people helped this book become what it is, and I'm beyond thankful to all of them.

Special thanks to:

My Kieran—every single person who gets to spend a portion of their days with you is beyond lucky; including me. You are in everything I write, and I am constantly inspired by your generosity, your kindness, and your courage. I want to be you when I grow up.

My grandfather, Besten—I like to think you'd be pleased to know that, twenty years later, I still attribute my writing voice to the Åsta Holth books you handed me when I was fourteen, the very ones that are now on my shelf. And even though *The Norwegian Christmas Marriage Plot* won't make it into your extensive library, there's another book in the world because of you.

My grandmother, Farmor—you never received your Christmas gift in 2020, but we got the gift of you, for eighty-six years, and I got thirty-one of those, and for that, I'm forever grateful. The national costumes in this book are inspired by the one you sewed for me for my confirmation, and I will forever cherish this piece of you still here.

My grandfather, Morfar—I think of you every time I sit down to write, and your pride in my books is still my source of encouragement. You may not be here in the flesh where we'd like you most, but you are *here with us* all the same.

My grandmother, Mormor—I could never be who I am without you. I can't wait to hug you again, and there will never be a time when your hugs don't remind me of sunscreen, summer, and home. Thank you for being my very best friend.

My favorite duck, Jenni Sauer—for being absolute trash for these two forever and always.

My world treasure, Tara Knott—for making room for my little family in your big, big heart. There's nothing I can write here that will really explain how very much we love and appreciate you.

Amanda Thornell—for being my safe space.

Lauren Wyant—for teaching me all there is to know about life on the Southside of Texas. I owe you my sanity.

My Virtual Roommate, Ingjerd Løvgren Auestad—for all the things. We have a house! With a view of the woods and birches! And a housekeeper!

Stian—it is hard to get decent help in the house these days. Thank you for understanding that literally every day is Ingjerd Appreciation Day; you will always be my favorite for that.

My editor, Savanna Roberts—for making it possible for me to do this. I honestly would not publish if it wasn't for you. Your editing skills, pterodactyl screeches, and faith in my stories are unparalleled, and your friendship means the world to me. Thank you!

Penny McIntosh—for loving this book and prompting me to rewrite it in the first place.

My sister, Ingvild—for telling me you'd definitely read a full-length novel about Ragnhild and Thorleif. You have one now.

My brother, Per—for baking only gingersnap pigs that year, bringing the *lussekatt* crocodile into existence, and for patiently walking me through tax terms, emigration laws, university applications, and other things my brain refuses to understand.

My ARC readers—for taking time out of your busy schedules to read and review my story, and giving it the very best chance in a publishing world brimming with talent.

Marie, our imaginary kitchen maid—for always leaving me to clean up the kitchen. Actually, thanks for nothing, Marie.

ABOUT THE AUTHOR

AUSTIN RYAN was born and raised in Norway, and though she has never personally staged a wedding with her childhood best friend, she accidentally wrote a book filled to the brim with all the Christmas traditions and foods of her upbringing. The Norwegian Christmas Marriage Plot, based on her 2020 novella by (almost) the same name, is her fourth full-length novel.

Austin lives with her family in Connecticut, surrounded by bookshelves and faerie lights, and plenty of scope for the imagination. When she's not editing for other authors, getting lost in their stories, or writing her own, you can find her on adventures with her favorite son—in the woods back home, in airports around the world, and the pages of books old and new.

CONNECT WITH AUSTIN RYAN

Website: www.authoraustinryan.com
Facebook: www.facebook.com/AuthorAustinRyan
Instagram: www.instagram.com/authoraustinryan
Amazon: www.amazon.com/Austin-Ryan/e/B08PPWX9KB
Goodreads: www.goodreads.com/austinryan

www.ingramcontent.com/pod-product-compliance
Lightning Source LLC
Chambersburg PA
CBHW031229260626
47169CB00007B/2211